The closeness, the gentleness, the passion, the hunger. She remembered all of it.

Because Gus, damn it, was back in her life.

And she, fool that she was, had let him in. She'd gone to dinner with him. She'd gone to childbirth class with him.

Next thing you knew, she'd be giving her heart to him.

No. Oh, no. Not again…

Dear Reader,

Our 20th anniversary pledge to you, our devoted readers, is a promise to continue delivering passionate, powerful, provocative love stories from your favorite Silhouette Desire authors for all the years to come!

As an anniversary treat, we've got a special book for you from the incomparable Annette Broadrick. *Marriage Prey* is a romance between the offspring of two couples from Annette's earliest Desire books, which Silhouette reissued along with a third early Desire novel last month as *Maximum Marriage: Men on a Mission.* Bestselling author Mary Lynn Baxter brings you November's MAN OF THE MONTH…*Her Perfect Man.* A minister and a reformed party girl fall for each other in this classic opposites-attract love story. *A Cowboy's Gift* is the latest offering by RITA Award winner Anne McAllister in her popular CODE OF THE WEST miniseries.

Another RITA winner, Caroline Cross, delivers the next installment of the exciting Desire miniseries FORTUNE'S CHILDREN: THE GROOMS with *Husband—or Enemy?* Dixie Browning's miniseries THE PASSIONATE POWERS continues with *The Virgin and the Vengeful Groom,* part of our extra-sensual BODY & SOUL promotion. And Sheri WhiteFeather has created another appealing Native American hero in *Night Wind's Woman.*

So please join us in celebrating twenty glorious years of category romance by indulging yourself with all six of these compelling love stories from Silhouette Desire!

Enjoy!

Joan Marlow Golan

Joan Marlow Golan
Senior Editor, Silhouette Desire

Please address questions and book requests to:
Silhouette Reader Service
U.S.: 3010 Walden Ave., P.O. Box 1325, Buffalo, NY 14269
Canadian: P.O. Box 609, Fort Erie, Ont. L2A 5X3

A Cowboy's Gift
ANNE McALLISTER

Published by Silhouette Books
America's Publisher of Contemporary Romance

If you purchased this book without a cover you should be aware
that this book is stolen property. It was reported as "unsold and
destroyed" to the publisher, and neither the author nor the
publisher has received any payment for this "stripped book."

In memory of our very own
D. A. "Gus" Hazel
1854-1880
and for Goliath,
you were the best

SILHOUETTE BOOKS

ISBN 0-373-76329-8

A COWBOY'S GIFT

Copyright © 2000 by Barbara Schenck

All rights reserved. Except for use in any review, the reproduction
or utilization of this work in whole or in part in any form by any
electronic, mechanical or other means, now known or hereafter
invented, including xerography, photocopying and recording, or in
any information storage or retrieval system, is forbidden without
the written permission of the editorial office, Silhouette Books,
300 East 42nd Street, New York, NY 10017 U.S.A.

All characters in this book have no existence outside the imagination of
the author and have no relation whatsoever to anyone bearing the same
name or names. They are not even distantly inspired by any individual
known or unknown to the author, and all incidents are pure invention.

This edition published by arrangement with Harlequin Books S.A.

® and TM are trademarks of Harlequin Books S.A., used under license.
Trademarks indicated with ® are registered in the United States Patent
and Trademark Office, the Canadian Trade Marks Office and in other
countries.

Visit Silhouette at www.eHarlequin.com

Printed in U.S.A.

Books by Anne McAllister

Silhouette Desire

*Cowboys Don't Cry #907
*Cowboys Don't Quit #944
*Cowboys Don't Stay #969
*The Cowboy and the Kid #1009
*Cowboy Pride #1034
*The Cowboy Steals a Lady #1117
*The Cowboy Crashes a Wedding #1153
*The Stardust Cowboy #1219
*A Cowboy's Secret #1279
*A Cowboy's Gift #1329

Silhouette Special Edition

*A Cowboy's Tears #1137

*Code of the West

Silhouette Books

World's Most Eligible Bachelors
*Cowboy on the Run

ANNE McALLISTER

RITA Award-winning author Anne McAllister fell in
love with a cowboy when she was five years old. Tall,
dark, handsome lone-wolf types have appealed to her
ever since. "Me, for instance," her college professor husband says. Well, yes. But even though she's been married
to the man of her dreams for over thirty years, she still
likes writing about those men of the West! And even
though she may take a break from cowboy heroes now
and then, she has lots more stories planned for the CODE
OF THE WEST. She is always happy to hear from readers, and if you'd like, you can write to Anne at P.O. Box
3904, Boseman, Montana 59772. SASE appreciated.

IT'S OUR 20th ANNIVERSARY!
We'll be celebrating all year,
Continuing with these fabulous titles,
On sale in November 2000.

Desire

#1327 Marriage Prey
Annette Broadrick

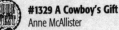

#1328 Her Perfect Man
Mary Lynn Baxter

#1329 A Cowboy's Gift
Anne McAllister

#1330 Husband—or Enemy?
Caroline Cross

#1331 The Virgin and the Vengeful Groom
Dixie Browning

#1332 Night Wind's Woman
Sheri WhiteFeather

Romance

#1480 Her Honor-Bound Lawman
Karen Rose Smith

#1481 Raffling Ryan
Kasey Michaels

#1482 The Millionaire's Waitress Wife
Carolyn Zane

#1483 The Doctor's Medicine Woman
Donna Clayton

#1484 The Third Kiss
Leanna Wilson

#1485 The Wedding Lullaby
Melissa McClone

Special Edition

#1357 A Man Alone
Lindsay McKenna

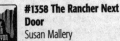

#1358 The Rancher Next Door
Susan Mallery

#1359 Sophie's Scandal
Penny Richards

#1360 The Bridal Quest
Jennifer Mikels

#1361 Baby of Convenience
Diana Whitney

#1362 Just Eight Months Old...
Tori Carrington

Intimate Moments

#1039 The Brands Who Came for Christmas
Maggie Shayne

#1040 Hero at Large
Robyn Amos

#1041 Made for Each Other
Doreen Owens Malek

#1042 Hero for Hire
Marie Ferrarella

#1043 Dangerous Liaisons
Maggie Price

#1044 Dad in Blue
Shelley Cooper

One

D. A. "Gus" Holt had never stayed still for more than five minutes in his entire life.

From the moment the doc had smacked his bottom in the hospital thirty-one years ago, Gus had been a goer, a doer—a hell-bent-for-mischief little boy who'd grown up into a hard-driving, hard-riding, hard-living, bronc-ridin' cowpoke.

The road didn't exist that Gus hadn't been down. The bronc didn't buck that he hadn't rode—or at the very least tried.

Gus was known for his try—that almost mystical blend of cowboy guts and will—which, when combined with God-given bullheadedness and Gus's occasional determined stupidity, had over the years helped him accomplish almost any damn thing he chose.

It had kept him competing in spite of three broken ribs and a dislocated shoulder the first year he'd had a chance

to go to Vegas for the National Finals. It had brought him
out of the hospital with his ankle in a cast to win in the
short-go two years ago at Cheyenne. It had helped him
drive eleven-hundred miles in way less time than the high-
way patrol would have approved of to make his ride on
Ground Zero, the best bucking horse of the year, in Pen-
dleton a year ago September.

It had kept him going for a dozen years.

But it wasn't helping now—because for the first time in
thirty-one years, Gus didn't have a goal.

He was drifting, lost, a ship without a rudder, a compass
with no sense of north.

For the first time ever, Gus didn't know what he wanted
or where he was headed. Worse, he didn't even know how
it had happened.

He only knew he didn't have the desire anymore.

And he didn't even have an excuse.

Lots of rodeo cowboys lost their careers to injury. They
woke up in a hospital with a doctor telling them they'd
better find another line of work. Others hung up their spurs
when they finished first. They won their gold buckle and,
satisfied, they bowed out.

Gus had had his share of injuries and docs telling him
he'd be better off doing something else. But he'd never
agreed with them, and he'd always fought to come back.
He'd won his share of gold buckles, including the big one
that everyone wanted. Three years ago he'd been the PRCA
bronc-riding champion of the world. But even after he'd
won it, he'd kept right on competing because he still had
the drive, he still had the fire and the desire.

And now he didn't.

Just like that.

Well, no, maybe not just like that.

It didn't—bang!—vanish the way a tire popped. Nope.

This was more like a slow leak. And, if he was honest, it had been going on for a while, sneaking inside his life, settling in and taking hold before he really realized it was there.

He began to see it in little things. All those miles he drove had seemed longer this year. The satisfaction of an eighty-eight-point ride didn't feel as good.

He didn't bounce up when he was down the way he used to. He creaked a little more when he got up in the morning, and it took him longer to work the kinks out.

He might have felt more juiced if he'd been going to the Finals this year. Then he'd have had a goal at least.

But for the first time in eight years, he wasn't going. Breaking his wrist in Dodge City this August had pretty much ended the possibility of that.

He'd vowed to come back for a couple of rides at the end of the season. It was the standard, acceptable thing to say. And the day money might have been worth it if he'd won.

But his wrist didn't feel real strong come mid-October, and the doc told him he'd be crazy to risk it.

Being told he was crazy had never stopped Gus before. This time it did.

And when Noah Tanner and Taggart Jones invited him to teach some classes at their bronc-riding school in Elmer, he'd skipped Minot and the Cow Palace and had gone to Elmer instead.

That's when he realized something was seriously screwy. When a hell-raiser like him thought *teaching school*—even bronc-riding school—was preferable to giving his all in the rodeo arena, something wasn't adding up.

He wasn't complaining exactly. He wasn't unhappy.

He was just wondering where he was going with his life, what the point was.

Deep stuff for a guy who pretty much wrote the book on being shallow.

He'd come to Taggart's, figuring he'd get it all sorted out and take off again in a week or so. But he hadn't.

He'd been here close to a month now, teaching three-and four-day clinics and helping with the ranch work the rest of the time. And he was no nearer understanding himself or what he wanted than he had been four weeks before.

He felt like he was standing still, waiting for something to happen.

It was happening—just not to him.

It had been a shock and a half to find out that his brother, J.D., was getting married the weekend after next. And to Lydia Cochrane, for crying out loud!

Gus hadn't ever figured J.D. for the marrying type. Over the years J.D. had gone through girlfriends the way Taggart's best bull went through heifers, and he sure hadn't given any sign of settling on one—until all of a sudden Lydia nailed him down.

Gus wondered what the hell a woman like Lydia—a smart, city-girl lawyer—saw in a stubborn son-of-a-buck like his big brother.

After all, J.D. wasn't near as good-looking as Gus was. Didn't have near the charm, either, no matter what all those old girlfriends might say.

No sir, J.D. was just damn lucky.

And that was another thing going wrong with his head!

Here he was thinking his brother was *lucky* 'cause he was getting married!

For heaven's sake, if he'd thought marrying was so all-fired wonderful, Gus knew he could've been married by now himself.

For a dozen years, as a matter of fact.

If he'd wanted to be. *If* he hadn't come to his senses in time. *If* he hadn't told Mary it wouldn't work out because he wasn't ready to settle down like some old man. Well, actually, if he hadn't said he'd be better off dead than getting married in a week's time.

He probably shouldn't have said that.

Mary hadn't taken it real well.

Cripes, what was he doing, thinking about Mary?

He *never* thought about Mary.

Well, almost never.

There was no point. He hadn't seen his ex-fiancée in years. Last he'd heard she'd moved to Arizona, had intended to go to college down there. That had been a long time ago.

Arizona? College?

Mary?

Go figure, Gus thought as he prowled around the bunkhouse on the Jones ranch. All he knew was he had way too much time on his hands if he was thinking about her.

Sometimes, when he'd been down in Scottsdale or Tucson or Window Rock riding broncs, Mary had crossed his mind, and he'd find himself wondering if she might come and watch him ride—for old-time's sake.

He actually remembered daydreaming once or twice— after a couple of the rodeos he'd won—that she would come looking for him, that she'd come right up and slide her arms around him and tuck her hands in his back pockets the way she used to and kiss him like he'd never been kissed before. Or since.

It was not restful, thinking things like that.

And there he was again, thinking about *restful!*

Decidedly rest*less,* Gus kept pacing. Since when had he ever cared about *restful?* Well, he hadn't. Still didn't.

But that was what happened when you were stuck in the middle of nowhere for weeks on end with nothing to do.

He should've gone into Elmer tonight with some of the cowboys who'd come for the bull-riding school.

The Dew Drop wasn't exactly your Million-Dollar Cowboy Bar, but he could've shot some pool, drunk some beer, maybe set his sights on a little gal who was as lonesome as he was.

Was he lonesome?

Was that what was wrong with him? Gus flung himself down on the narrow wood-frame bed and considered the possibility.

He couldn't ever remember being lonesome in his life. Hell, he'd never been *alone* in his life! He'd always had his brother or his buddies or a whole bevy of women to keep him occupied. Lonesome?

No, he wasn't lonesome. He was just…just…

Hell! He bounced back up off the bed. All this soul-searching wasn't gettin' him anywhere! He needed noise! People! Action!

It was only ten o'clock. Still early. The Dew Drop wouldn't start rocking for another hour.

He yanked a clean shirt out of the closet, tugged it on, buttoned it up, tucked it in. Then he buffed his cuff against his gold belt buckle, shrugged into his sheepskin jacket and clapped his black winter Stetson on his head.

He felt better already. Full of purpose.

Whatever he found at the Dew Drop had to be better than this!

He found cigarettes and smoke and a little honky-tonk music. Half a dozen local cowpokes lounged at the bar. More were playing cards and shooting pool. Two of the bull riders from Taggart's were playing pool, too. Three others, ones who'd had to peel themselves off the arena dirt quick this afternoon, were drowning their aches and pains in bottles of beer. A couple of buckle bunnies were chatting them up. Another had her arm looped through bull rider, Steve Hammond's, arm. They were heading out as Gus came in.

Steve gave Gus a thumbs-up as they passed.

"Don't do nothin' I wouldn't do," Gus said.

Steve grinned. "No fear." Then he turned to the woman on his arm. "Not much ol' Gus wouldn't do."

That was a fact. Gus grinned as the door banged shut behind him.

"Hey, Gus!" One of the bull-rider pool players waved him over. "Wanta play doubles?"

He snagged a beer, grabbed a pool cue and joined them. He tried to get interested. Gus did everything competitively, but it was hard to concentrate when everybody but him shot pool with one eye on the girls who came to watch.

When a couple of the girls put their quarters on the table for the next game, he had hopes that it might get interesting, but it didn't. They didn't play well. They just batted their lashes and flirted, and his buddies flirted right back.

Gus had done the same thing himself a thousand other times. It hadn't ever annoyed him before. It annoyed him tonight.

He tried flirting, too, but he couldn't seem to get into it. His smiles felt forced. His teasing jokes sounded as flat to his ear as the beer tasted on his tongue.

When one of the girls said, "Maybe you'd rather dance, sweetheart," he gave it a shot. But the music sounded flat, too.

Maybe he was getting sick.

But before he could decide if he was running a fever, one of the locals decided he didn't want Gus that close to his girl.

"I ain't your girl, Tommy," the girl said.

But Tommy had had enough alcohol to believe other-wise. "I said, take your hands offa' her." And he followed his words with his fist.

Well, hell, Gus thought, his head snapping back with the force of the blow, this was more like it!

He swung back, felt the solid crack of his fist against the local cowboy's jaw.

"Git 'im, Gus!"

"C'mon, Tom!"

After that it was pretty much a free-for-all.

Twenty minutes, one black eye and two loose teeth later, Gus was on his way back to the ranch. And even though he was pretty sure it was one of the bull riders, not Tommy, who had given him the shiner and the loose teeth, he didn't complain.

Hell, no.

A guy felt alive when he came out swinging.

Leastways, Gus thought with a sigh, he always used to.

"Nice shiner." Taggart studied Gus's eye with interest when Gus showed up at the house for breakfast the next morning. "Didn't realize that bronc you were 'demonstrat-ing' on yesterday nailed you."

"Didn't," Gus muttered. He slid into the chair beside Becky, Taggart's daughter.

"What happened?" she asked, her eyes wide with worry.

Gus shrugged awkwardly. "Ran into a door," he mum-bled. He shouldn't have come up for breakfast. He should've known better. But he hadn't given it much thought this morning, even though three or four of the guys had remarked on how good a time he must have had last night.

In the old days Gus would've grinned and agreed with

them. This morning he'd just shrugged on his way up to Taggart's house.

He came every morning for breakfast. "It's part of the deal," Taggart had told him when he'd first arrived. "Home cookin' is part of your wages. You're welcome to eat with us anytime."

At first Gus had come because Taggart's wife, Felicity, was a darn good cook, and home-cooked meals were pretty much a novelty in his life.

So, it turned out, was being part of a family, hunting up lost-at-the-last-minute math books for Becky and cutting toast into skinny "firewood logs" for Willy and Abby, the three-year-old twins, and listening to all the chatter. He figured he'd get sick of it darn fast and make do with the coffee and doughnuts the other cowboys went after.

But he'd been coming up to the house for breakfast all month as well as for dinner. He actually liked it.

"You should've put ice on it right away." Felicity studied his eye as she set a plate of bacon and eggs in front of him. "We always have plenty. It's an occupational necessity in these parts."

"Did you do it last night? You could have called. I would've brought you some ice," Becky said eagerly.

Becky was all eagerness these days, and as devoted to Gus as Gus was to breakfast.

He was still trying to come to terms with her as a teenager.

She sure didn't look like the little kid he remembered. She reached his chin now and had this amazing long straight brown hair. Before Taggart had married Felicity, he'd always kept it chopped short because, he said, it was a whole lot easier to take care of.

Now it was long and thick and reminded Gus of Dallas Cowboys cheerleaders' hair. There was a terrifying thought.

Even more terrifying was realizing that even though Becky didn't have the shape of a Cowboys cheerleader yet, there were definite signs of curves in a shape he remembered as fence-post straight when she'd been a little girl.

The realization made him feel awkward. And old.

Now he glanced sideways at her sitting next to him at the table and said gruffly, "I ain't such an old man that I couldn't have hobbled up here and got some ice if I'd needed it. My eye's fine. I can still see through it. I can see you got oatmeal on your chin."

Hastily Becky wiped at her face. She looked flustered. The tips of her ears turned red.

"I was just kiddin'," he said after a moment, not wanting to have made her uncomfortable.

"Oh!" Becky brightened at once, then flashed him a thousand-watt smile. "That's okay, then." She dug into her oatmeal eating again. Her elbow bumped his. "Oops."

"You don't want to go to J.D.'s wedding with a black eye," Felicity decided.

Gus didn't want to go to J.D.'s wedding at all. Weddings had never been his thing. He'd shied away from them completely since…since he'd ducked out on his own.

"I'll get some ice." Becky shoved back her chair so quickly it tipped over. She scrambled to right it. "Sorry," she said again. Now her cheeks were red, too.

Gus wondered when she'd developed this inability to walk through a room without knocking over furniture. He'd thought that was the province of teenage boys.

Sighing, Becky finished wrapping the ice in a plastic bag and a dish towel. "Here." She poked it at Gus's eye. He reached for it. Their hands collided. The ice fell into his lap.

"Ohmigod! I'm sorry! I—"

Gus grabbed for the bag as the ice scattered everywhere. "It's okay. No sweat."

But Becky, her face now scarlet, dropped to her knees to begin picking it up. Willy and Abby plunged beneath the table to help.

"Let them do it," Taggart said, dragging Becky to her feet. "We gotta go."

Becky stumbled up, looking and not quite looking at Gus. "I didn't mean... Well, I...I hope your eye's better, Gus."

He flashed her a grin. "Don't worry about me. No damage really. See you later."

Becky swallowed and flashed him another thousand-watt smile. "Yeah. Right. That'd be great."

Taggart hauled her out the door.

"Beck's going through just a little bit of an awkward phase," Felicity said.

Gus blinked. "Is she?"

Well, she wasn't the only one.

His lack of intensity bothered him.

He puzzled over it all day long. All the time he was talking about muscle memory and focus to a bunch of green, bronc-rider wannabes, he tried to figure out why they had so much drive and he didn't.

Where had it gone?

Did it just evaporate? Was that normal?

He asked Noah Tanner while they were eating chili at lunch. "Did you just sorta lose it one day?" After all, Noah had once been bronc-riding champion of the world, too.

"Lose it?" Noah frowned.

"Wantin' to ride. It matterin' if you rode. I know you had the accident and it changed things..." Everyone in rodeo remembered the car wreck right after Noah and Taggart both won gold buckles at the NFR. They'd retired a few months later. "But before that…did you ever feel…I don't know…like there was somethin' missing?"

Noah shook his head. "Nope."

But Taggart said, "Yeah," and Gus looked at him hopefully. "Becky," Taggart said. "I was busy runnin' around, and she wasn't there."

"Maybe you've got a kid somewhere," Noah said cheerfully. "Like I did."

His daughter, Susannah, had been a big surprise to Noah when, seven years after the fact, he'd found out he was a dad.

"God, I hope not!" Gus felt as if he'd been punched.

But it was sure something to think about. He started wondering—and worrying. There had been women since Mary. He couldn't deny it. But he'd been careful—always—to be sure that both he and the lady in question were protected. He wasn't worried about them.

But what if Mary had—

No, she couldn't!

Besides, he'd already asked. He actually called her from Reno one night when a cowboy buddy of his was reeling from the news that he was going to be a father, and he'd asked her point-blank. "Are you pregnant?"

She'd said, "Who is this?" like she didn't know!

Like she slept with guys all the time, which ticked him off royally, but he'd ignored it. He'd said, "I just wanted you to know, I'd marry you if you were."

She hadn't pretended not to know who he was then. She'd said, "Go to hell, Gus."

Which he had taken to mean she wasn't.

And he'd breathed easier. He'd been breathing easier for a lot of years. But he remembered that Tess hadn't told Noah.

What if Mary hadn't bothered to tell him?

What if there was a kid—a kid almost as old as Becky!—walking around looking like him? What if—

He shoved his bowl of chili away. ''I don't feel so good.''

He went outside and took deep lungfuls of crisp November mountain air. He tried to think logically and rationally about the gut-twisting emotion that just grabbed him at Noah's words.

Could Mary have had a kid?

Surely she would have told him? Wouldn't she? Wouldn't she have called J.D. and told him to have Gus call her? Wouldn't she have tracked him to the ends of the earth?

Of course she would have, he assured himself.

Mary had loved him. She wouldn't have kept a secret like that.

He hoped.

He was still wrestling with the question, though, when Noah gave a whistle. ''Time for class.''

He spent the afternoon talking about mechanics, about isolating movements, about what happened when you made a mistake and then another and another.

He didn't feel like he was talking about bronc riding.

Cripes, maybe he'd been in one place too long, he thought as he watched the last of his bronc riders do another ride. Maybe he was going stir crazy, spending too much time in one place. Maybe after the wedding he ought to hit the road, go down south, get a little sun, try his hand at a couple of Arizona rodeos.

''Hey, Gus?''

He turned to see Becky approaching.

''Are you armed?'' he asked, grinning.

She blushed. "What?" Then her cheeks reddened. "No," she muttered.

His grin widened at the color in her face. There was nothing Gus liked better than teasing a pretty girl, even a thirteen-year-old one. "What's up?"

"I was wondering if, uh…if maybe you could give me a ride in to school?"

"I thought you just got back from school."

"Well, I did. I, um, sorta forgot. I'm supposed to be practicing for a speech tournament. An' my teacher said she'd stay after school today to listen to us. But I was already on the bus and halfway home before I remembered."

"Sounds like you like school the way I used to."

"Oh, I like it," Becky said quickly. "Most of it. I like English. An' speech. I'm giving a speech about training Domino." That was the three-year-old gelding she and her dad were working on together.

"Wish they'd had subjects like that when I was in school," Gus said a little enviously. "I would've liked to give a speech on how to ride a bronc."

"You could have in my class. It's great. Eighth-grade speech. Did you know I'm going into high school next year?"

"Holy cow." He really did feel old. "Reckon I'll be goin' into a nursing home anyday."

"You will not! You're not old! I mean, well…you don't seem all that much older than me."

Gus hoped that was a compliment. He wasn't sure. So he asked more about Domino's training, and Becky talked enthusiastically about that as they drove into Elmer.

He pulled up in front of the school, and she opened the door, then turned to him. "I'll be about a half an hour." She pointed to a classroom on the first floor. "That's where

I'll be. You can meet me out here, though. I'll come out when I'm done.''

Gus cocked his head. "You mean I can't come listen?"

"You wouldn't want to do that!"

"I might learn something."

Becky hesitated, then she shrugged, too. "Well, if I'm not out in forty-five minutes, come and get me. I'll be ready to go by then."

"I thought you said you liked this class."

"I do. But I've got a life, you know. An' I wouldn't want to keep you waiting. Maybe we could get a Coke when I finish. I'll pay," she said quickly, cheeks flushed. "I mean, 'cause I invited you."

Gus laughed. "I think I can spring for a couple of Cokes. I'm gonna run a couple of errands for your folks. If you're not out when I get back, I'll come in and get you."

Becky beamed. "See you!" She took off toward the school at a run, then stopped abruptly and, with a quick glance back, continued on, this time walking as sedately as you please.

He looked around to see who she was trying to impress. There were a couple of boys tossing a football on the lawn and surreptitiously watching Becky. He grinned, remembering what it was like. Back then it had been simple. It seemed like another life.

He picked up the baling wire Taggart had ordered from the hardware store. He stopped at the grocery store and got the stuff on Felicity's list. The clerk, whose name tag said Kitzy, had been in the bar last night. She fussed over his black eye.

"I could kiss it and make it better," she offered, batting her lashes at him.

Since Kitzy snapped her gum and kept the eye-shadow people in business, Gus wasn't even tempted. Gus rubbed the back of his neck and side-stepped toward the door. "I'm in sort of a hurry."

"You could come by my place this evenin', sugar," Kitzy said. "When you're not in such an all-fired rush."

Gus shot her a fleeting grin. "Don't think so," he muttered, grabbing the milk and bread and heading for the door.

It was time to pick up Becky, anyway. He stowed the stuff in the back and headed over to the school. Becky wasn't out front so he parked the truck, hopped out and strode in.

The smells of chalk dust, varnish and old gym shoes washed over him. He hadn't been in a school since he'd graduated. It felt like yesterday—and like a hundred years ago.

As a boy he'd chafed under the demands of education. He'd wanted to be out, gone, graduated, on his way.

To what?

At the time it had seemed so clear. And now...hell, now he supposed he ought to be wherever he'd been heading.

And he didn't even know where that was!

His footsteps quickened as he headed toward the classroom Becky had pointed out. His boots clicked on the linoleum and echoed in the empty hall. At the far end in one of the classrooms, he could hear a voice—youthful, female—speaking.

It was Becky, he could tell. Her voice was clear and strong and earnest. He reached the doorway and stopped. Becky stood at the front of the class, her notes spread before her, her fingers in a death grip on the podium. Then she looked up, and her voice faltered when she spied him.

Gus gave her a quick thumbs-up and an encouraging grin. "Go for it," he mouthed.

Becky nodded, took a deep breath and carried on. She

glanced at her notes once more, then lifted her gaze and talked to him this time, telling him about Domino, about how she was training him, about how *he* was training *her*.

It was a good speech. Hell, it was a terrific speech. Informative, clear and to the point. And when she finished, Gus stepped forward clapping enthusiastically.

When he stopped there was silence.

Everyone looked around—including Gus. Then he spotted the blond woman, Becky's teacher, he guessed, sitting at a table on the far side of the room.

Her face was stark white, very familiar, and a whole lot paler than he'd ever seen it. She was staring not at Becky, but at him.

"Gus?" she said hoarsely.

He opened his mouth in astonishment. *"Mary?"*

Two

As she said his name, Mary McLean felt a quick sharp blow to her midsection. And it might as well have been Gus—and not the baby doing somersaults in her abdomen—who had kicked her.

Of all the places she had ever considered she might run into Gus Holt in the past twelve years, an eighth-grade classroom in Elmer, Montana, didn't even make the list.

If it had, she would never have come.

She'd avoided every other place she might conceivably have run into the footloose cowboy who had dumped her all those years ago.

She'd left Murray as soon as she could after she'd canceled the wedding, sent back the gifts, burned the invitations.

She hadn't even set foot in Montana again until three months ago. She'd gone to Arizona to live with her sister, Ruthie, and Ruthie's husband, Jeff. She'd spent a dozen years in the Phoenix area, first in college and then teaching school. She'd been determined to be happy there. And she had been.

More or less.

She had come back this year to teach because she'd desperately needed some space. Her life had changed. And while she loved Ruthie and Jeff dearly, she hadn't wanted them hovering over her every minute.

Ruthie and Jeff hadn't been pleased. They'd argued with her. They'd fussed over her. She'd need them, they told her.

But Mary knew she would need her own life more.

"But the baby…" They'd argued.

Fortunately the doctor had been on her side. Once she had passed the first trimester successfully, he'd said she didn't have to remain nearby. She could go anywhere, he'd assured her. He'd understood her need to have her own life, to be on her own.

"But the baby…" Ruthie and Jeff had protested still.

But Mary hadn't knuckled under. She'd found this job in Elmer—and she had been determined to take it. To come back to Montana. To come home.

It was time. She was ready now. She was older, stronger, wiser. A far cry from the foolish young girl who had given her heart to Gus Holt.

Besides, it wasn't as if she was going back to Murray where she might have run into him when he came through town.

Montana was a big place.

"It will be good for me," she'd assured Ruthie and Jeff. "And you can come when the baby's due."

"We don't even know where Elmer is!" her sister had complained.

Neither had Mary then. She found out it was nestled

against the foothills on the western edge of the Shields Valley north of Livingston. When she'd arrived, the stunning views and high mountain air made her feel alive and eager. Yes, she thought, it was right to come. She'd thought Elmer was the most perfect place on earth.

Until now.

Until Gus. What on earth was Gus doing *here?*

She wanted to know.

She *didn't* want to ask.

She certainly didn't want to care!

More than anything, she wanted to be polite and professional and determinedly distant to the man who had once upon a time turned her life upside down.

She'd thought she could be.

She'd been determined she would be. Periodically over the years, she'd anticipated the moment she would run into Gus again. She'd imagined how cool and dismissive and indifferent she'd be.

After all, she wasn't a dreamy teenager anymore. She was a woman now—grown-up, professional, mature.

The naive girl who had dreamed of weddings and honeymoons and happily-ever-afters had been buried a long, long time ago.

Gus had taken care of that when he'd called her from Cheyenne a week before their wedding to tell her he couldn't go through with it.

"I'm not ready to get married," he'd said without preamble.

Mary, counting the days, then in the single digits until the wedding, had been stunned, sure she hadn't heard him right.

"What did you say?" she'd asked faintly. "What?"

So he'd repeated it. "I can't do it. I got places to go,

things to do. When I think about settlin' down, I get...I don't know...this chokin' feeling.''

"Choking feeling?"

And while she'd clutched the telephone and stammered her astonishment—he'd been the one to propose, after all, hadn't he!—he'd not only buried her heart, he'd nailed the lid down on the coffin of her dreams.

"It doesn't mean I don't love you, Mary," he'd said earnestly. "It's just I figure I might as well be dead as married right now."

She hadn't told her parents that! She hadn't told anyone that Gus had thought he might as well be dead as married to her.

She'd said Gus had had "second thoughts." She'd said he felt he wasn't ready. She said it calmly and carefully and dispassionately. She'd even said she thought he was right. Certainly if he felt death was better than being married, she didn't want to marry him, either!

And then she'd set about calling it off.

While Gus had gone right on down the road—"alive" once more, Mary, dying inside, had called the minister, notified the guests, sent back the presents. She'd taken the tiny diamond Gus had given her and had given it to his brother to return to him.

"I'm sorry, Mary." J.D. had looked miserable.

No more miserable than Mary felt.

"Poor Mary," everyone said after that. She'd been the one who'd been dumped. She'd been the one who'd had to face the pitying looks and worried glances.

That had been bad.

What was worse was that she loved Gus—and he had broken her foolish young heart.

That was a dozen years ago, she reminded herself. *Eons ago. Another lifetime.*

It didn't matter now.

Gus didn't matter!

Now she sat at the table and clenched her grade book against her like a shield, and prayed it would protect her from his lethal charm. He still had it—she could see that across the room.

He came toward her, a wide grin and a black eye—some things never changed!—on his damnably handsome face. It was older and craggier now, but no less gorgeous. She wanted to look away, but she couldn't.

"My God, Mary! What're you doin' here? How are you? My gosh, it's good to see you! Holy cow, it's been years!"

He gave every indication of being about to do what he'd always done when he'd come home—grabbing her, then sweeping her up into a breathtaking hug and kissing her till she was gasping for air.

The very thought froze Mary right where she was. She sat stone still and held out a polite hand.

"Hello, Gus," she said in quiet, well-modulated tones and was relieved to hear herself sound distant and polite.

He stared at her, then at her outstretched hand. His brows drew down in a frown. "Mar'? What's this?"

Resolutely she kept her hand right out there. *Shake it, damn you. We are acquaintances now. Nothing more.* She met his gaze stubbornly.

Finally Gus shrugged. He rubbed his right hand against the side of his jeans and took hold of hers. His palm was callused, hard, slightly rough, and Mary remembered, without wanting to, the times it had touched her bare flesh.

Something kicked over inside her, and she didn't think it was the child. She tried to jerk her hand away.

Gus held on. His hard, warm fingers wrapped hers. Short of fighting him for possession, she had no recourse but to leave her hand in his.

He was still grinning at her, that lopsided, crooked grin she used to love so much. "Mary, Mary. You are a sight for sore eyes."

"Which you have, I see," she said tartly, steeling herself against the grin. Against *him!*

Gus, still grinning, touched his eye. "Just got on the wrong side of a fist. No big deal."

No. It never was. Gus and J.D. had taken on all comers back when they were growing up. Mary's mother had always called them "those roughneck Holt boys," as in, "Stay away from those roughneck Holt boys."

But Mary, foolish Mary, had fallen in love with Gus.

"I can't believe it's you. I've been thinking about you lately!" He crowed with delight while her students looked on with interest.

"I can't imagine why," Mary said curtly. "I haven't been thinking about you. Ah, Sam!"

Thank God. One of Becky's classmates, Sam Bacon, was slouched in the doorway, waiting to give his speech and looking as though he wished he were anywhere but here.

Mary knew exactly how he felt. "Come in! Come in!"

She managed to jerk her hand out of Gus's grasp at last and wave Sam into the room. "Just in time. Becky's all finished and her ride is here. They were just leaving."

She beckoned once more to Sam and was relieved to see him slink forward into the room.

"Good job," she said briskly to Becky, looking right past Gus. "That last run-through was terrific. Much better eye contact. Do it like that in Bozeman and you'll make us all proud."

Becky beamed and slanted a quick glance in Gus's direction. It was a starry-eyed, hungry glance, and it reminded Mary all too well of the way she had once looked at him.

Gus didn't seem to notice. He was still looking at her. "Hey, Mar', how about—"

"It was nice to see you again." Then she turned all her attention on Sam. "Go right on up to the podium. I'm ready when you are."

"Mary—" Gus wasn't moving away.

"I'm afraid you'll have to excuse me, Gus. I've got work to do. Sam," she said pointedly. "I'm waiting."

Sam reached the podium and jammed his hands into his pockets, then rocked back on his heels.

"Well, when you're not busy—" Gus persisted.

"I'm always busy. Sam? They take points off if you don't begin promptly."

"You can't be *always* busy!" Gus protested.

She'd be busy forever, Mary vowed, keeping her eyes fixed on Sam. "Becky's waiting, Gus." *Why in heaven's name wouldn't the kid start?* "Let's get going, Sam. It's getting late. I'm listening."

But Sam, who had been watching Gus's attempts to get her attention, gave her a look that said clearly that he didn't think she was listening at all and he was willing to wait.

Becky shouldered her backpack. "Come on, Gus. I thought we were gonna get a Coke."

Mary could feel his frustration. She'd always known what Gus was feeling—or she'd always thought she had.

She apparently hadn't known he thought marrying her would kill him. But about other, less vital, things, she'd known him well. She knew he wanted to grab her and her attention now.

But she wasn't going to let him. She stared determinedly at Sam. She tapped her pencil. "Sam."

"Oh, hell. Er, heck. Fine. Let's go," Gus said to Becky. Out of the corner of her eye, she saw him take off his hat and rub his hand through his hair, then set it back on his head and tug it down tight.

He turned to follow Becky out of the room, then stopped and looked down at her. "I'll be back."

Mary was here! In Elmer, of all places!

Teaching school just miles from where he was living. For the past two months, she'd been just down the road! Gus couldn't believe it. He practically drove right past the tiny café he was so busy thinking and grinning like a polecat in a chicken coop.

"Gus?" Becky's voice, impatient and irritable, broke into the whirl of thoughts in his head. "Gus! Stop!"

He jammed on the brakes. "Sorry. Thinkin' about something."

Thinking about how damn fine Mary looked. A dozen years had made her more beautiful than ever. Her hair, still long and blonde, was pulled back and anchored neatly at the nape of her neck the way it had always been. And Gus couldn't help remembering how he'd loved loosening it, running his fingers through it, tousling it. He'd loved kissing those lips, too—those wonderful lips that had scowled at him today. He wondered how long it would take him to make her smile, to make that dimple at the corner of her mouth appear, to make—

"The café's right here."

"Huh?"

"I thought we were going to get a Coke," Becky reminded him.

"Oh. Right. Yeah, sure." Gus parked the truck outside the café. He hopped out, slapped his hand on the fender and then, still grinning, followed Becky in.

They took a table by the window, and Gus could see the

school from where he sat. If he craned his neck he could see Mary's classroom. He craned his neck.

"—really think it was okay?"

He jerked his attention back to Becky. "What?"

"What's the matter with you this afternoon? You haven't heard a word I've said. I said, did you really think my speech was okay?"

"It was great. Is your teacher new this year?"

"Miz McLean? Uh-huh. She's from Arizona. Do you know her?"

"Uh, yeah," he said absently. He was still stuck on Mary being *Miz* McLean. Like she was a grown-up. Hell, he guessed she was. She was Miz McLean. Did that make him Mr. Holt? It was a disconcerting thought.

He scratched his ear. "We go back a long way," he said after they'd ordered their drinks. "I knew her when I was a kid. Your age."

"I'm not a kid!" Becky looked offended.

"Right. Sorry. You're not," Gus backpedaled quickly. "Anyway, I reckon we were younger than you. In seventh grade."

God, yes. Seventh grade.

It had been years ago now. Nearly twenty. It felt like yesterday.

Becky dismissed seventh grade. It was beneath her. She talked about her speech and about Domino, about training him, about how maybe Gus could help. Gus didn't hear a word she said.

He was thinking about seventh grade. Thinking about the first day of junior high when he and Sloan Gallagher, his best friend, had been tossing Lydia Cochrane's book bag in a game of keep-away after school because it infuriated her—and Gus had always liked making Lydia mad.

He remembered how he'd grabbed the book bag when

Sloan tossed it to him. He'd taken off running. "Can't catch me!" he'd yelled, and darted around the corner of the school building, smacking straight into the prettiest girl he'd ever seen.

He'd knocked her flat.

In her own way—even as he'd stammered and apologized and turned beet-red as he'd helped her to her feet and had picked up her backpack and pens and notebooks— she'd knocked him flat, too.

She'd smiled at him—a little warily, true enough—but still she'd smiled. Even as she'd rubbed her scraped elbows, she'd said, "It's okay. Don't worry. I'm fine."

"You sure? You're kinda dusty." He'd started to swat the dirt and dust off the back of her jeans. But the moment his hand had come into contact with the soft, denim-covered curve of her body, he'd realized what he was doing and his face had flamed.

The rest of his body hadn't been exactly cool, either.

He'd been almost thirteen. Awkward. Unsure. Gangly, all of a sudden. And his body, which he'd understood and controlled really well for the first twelve years of his life, suddenly seemed to have developed interests of its own.

It had sure as heck been interested in the girl he'd just knocked into the dirt!

Sloan had come running up then, a furious Lydia on his heels.

"Hey!" Sloan yelled. "Let's get—oh!" And he'd stopped dead, too, at the sight of this beautiful blond girl covered with dirt.

"Oh, wow," he'd said after a minute. Then he'd just gaped. That was how pretty she'd been....

It wasn't all that unusual for Gus to be at a loss for words, but Sloan had never been tongue-tied in his life. Lydia, fortunately, wasn't.

"Are you okay?" She had taken the girl's backpack and was efficiently putting everything back in it again. "Don't mind them," she'd said dismissively. "They're idiots. I'm Lydia Cochrane."

The blond girl smiled. "Mary McLean," she'd said. "I'm new. We just moved here from Abilene."

"McLean? Your dad is the new principal?" Lydia had been delighted.

Gus had been appalled.

He'd just decked *the principal's daughter? The principal's daughter* made his heart pound and his palms sweat and his body do things it had no business doing!

Oh, God.

He remembered lowering Lydia's book bag and holding it strategically just below his belt, all the while hoping to heck Lydia and Mary McLean didn't notice the way his body was reacting.

The very thought of a girl being aware that she had that sort of effect on him made him want to sink right into the ground.

Funny how things changed.

A few years later he'd gloried in letting Mary see the kind of effect she'd had on him. He'd reveled in it.

He was a little surprised to find she'd had the same effect this afternoon.

"She didn't look real happy to see you," Becky said now through the straw of her Coke.

"She was probably surprised. She been teaching here long?"

Becky shook her head. "She's new this year. She got Miz Rasmussen's job when she retired. Thank heavens." Becky breathed a sigh of relief. "Miz Rasmussen taught my dad! Miz McLean's much better. Kinda strict, though. She doesn't put up with any nonsense."

"No?" Gus smiled. She'd put up with him.

He had been full of nonsense in those days. Once he'd got over his shock of being attracted to the principal's daughter, he'd been laughing and teasing and doing his best to get her goat whenever he could.

It was how a guy flirted when he was in junior high.

And Mary, who had always been lots more serious and sensible than he had, had been charmed.

People used to wonder what they saw in each other.

"Opposites attract," Mary had said breezily.

God knew Gus had been attracted to her.

He was always amazed that Mary had been attracted to him. But she must have been. She went to Murray's one picture show with him. She came out to his place and went riding with him. She sat with him on her porch swing and let him kiss her when no one was looking.

She became "Gus's girl."

And eventually pretty, steady, sensible Mary who never went off on wild-goose chases or chased rainbows, had done the wildest, most reckless thing of any girl he knew.

She'd got engaged to him!

It had shocked him when she'd said yes.

If Mary had been a strong, dependable anchor, Gus had been a kite, blowing in the wind, flying wild and free.

When they'd been together—from seventh grade on—it had always been fun. Dizzy, delightful fun. And when Gus had proposed, he'd thought he was proposing more fun— the only difference being that after they were married, they could have fun going down the road together.

It took him a while—because he hadn't got home very often—to figure out that Mary wasn't thinking like that at all.

She was thinking home and family. She was thinking cozy little ranch house and pink and blue baby blankets.

She was thinking about *her* dreams.

And they had nothing in common with *his*.

He couldn't be what she wanted him to be. And he knew it.

He'd fail her. He knew that, too.

He just hadn't known how to tell her. So he hadn't told her.

Mary was way smarter than he was. He reckoned she'd figure it out for herself.

He'd gone along with whatever she said, nodding and smiling every time he'd come home, and hitting the road again as fast as he could. He didn't want to hurt her, so he'd figured that if he didn't show much enthusiasm, she'd get the idea something was wrong and she'd have some second thoughts herself.

He'd wanted her to be the one to break it off. Wanted her to tell him he was too immature, too unsettled, too restless to be married. He'd wanted her to see what a mistake it was and then to cut him loose, to set him free.

But she'd never seen—except what she'd wanted to see.

And by the time Gus realized that she didn't know how really, really wrong it was, the wedding was only a week away—and he'd had to break it off himself.

He'd handled it badly. He'd never been great with words. And a long-distance phone call and a stack of quarters hadn't been the best way to tell her he couldn't go through with marrying her.

He supposed that accounted for her less-than-enthusiastic reception this afternoon.

He supposed he didn't blame her.

He couldn't imagine holding a grudge for a dozen years—hell, he barely remembered what happened yesterday—but, Mary...well, Mary was different.

Mary was thoughtful and kind and gentle and loving.

Mary had always taken everything to heart.

It was why he'd loved her.

This afternoon, when his heart kicked over and his stomach lurched at the mere sight of her, he had an intriguing thought—maybe he still did.

Well, it was over.

She'd seen Gus Holt—and had survived to tell the tale.

It hadn't been bad at all. Mary should have made a point to do it years ago, instead of putting it off, being afraid to see him again.

Piece of cake, that's what it had been.

It was just her clumsiness that had made her drop things this evening every time she heard a car in the street or every time there had been a knock on the door.

She'd been foolish expecting it to be Gus when first it had been Alice Benn, the retired schoolteacher who often came by in the evenings to chat, and then Mr. Eberhardt, bringing her a week's worth of *Chronicle*s.

Knowing Gus, he was probably already a hundred miles away.

That had been what he'd wanted, after all—his freedom. The open road. No ties. No wife. No family.

Mary still wondered how she could have been so wrong about him.

She didn't want to start thinking all over again about that. She'd thought that subject to death.

She'd attacked it from every angle, examined it every way and had finally come to terms with it. She'd even decided Gus was right—they shouldn't have gotten married. If he felt smothered, strangled, dead, they definitely shouldn't have gotten married!

But she'd loved him so much.

And even after all these years, it hurt.

This time when the knock came she only had a moment's qualm.

There was no way it was going to be Gus now. Even though it was late, chances were it was Cloris, the other retired schoolteacher in town. Cloris, close to eighty, lived alone and sometimes forgot what time it was when she had something she wanted to say.

Mary had answered the door to Cloris at five in the evening and five in the morning. Cloris had turned up at midnight once with a plate of homemade gingerbread, needing to share and just visit for a while.

Mary was brushing her teeth, ready for bed, but she wrapped her robe around her and opened the door.

Gus was standing there.

His hands were tucked in his pockets, and he was smiling at her with that same lopsided smile that had always made her insides turn to mush. He said, "Hey."

Mary swallowed and straightened. She bunched the robe firmly around her burgeoning belly and folded her arms across it. "Hey, yourself. It's after ten o'clock."

"It took me that long to get up the guts to come."

"You shouldn't have bothered," she said frostily, resisting his attempt to disarm her.

"You used to say you never cared what time I came."

Ah, damn it, why did he have to remember that. When she and Gus had been engaged and he'd been all over the map, she'd told him that anytime he was close, she'd want to see him, that it wouldn't matter what time it was.

"It's never too late, Gus," she'd told him, fool that she'd been.

"That was then," she said brusquely now, and tried to shut the door. It bumped hard against his boot, which was already planted on the threshold.

"Don't shut me out, Mary."

"Gus, I don't want—"

"Please," he said softly. "Don't."

And before she realized what he was about to do—before she could begin to stop him!—he stepped through the doorway, took her by the shoulders and planted his lips firmly and hungrily on hers.

Oh, God! Oh, help! Oh, no!

That was all Mary could think. She'd done her best to forget Gus—to forget his teasing, his laughter, his charm. But mostly she'd done her best to forget what it had been like to kiss Gus.

She'd refused to let herself dwell on memories of the hard warmth of his mouth, on the eager stroke of his tongue, on the way he had always been able to melt her right where she stood.

And that was why, earlier today, she'd believed she'd survived.

Because then he'd only grinned, he'd only talked.

He hadn't touched. Or kissed.

Oh, hell! she thought. Oh, damn. Oh...oh...oh, Gus, please go away!

But Gus didn't go. He stayed. And kissed her. Hungrily. Eagerly. Passionately.

The way he'd kissed her twelve years ago. The way he'd kissed her when she'd said yes, she'd marry him.

She jerked back away from him. "Damn it, Gus!"

He looked at her and grinned triumphantly. "There. See. Nothing's changed."

"Nothing's changed?" She gaped at him.

"Nope. Nothin' that matters."

Her jaw dropped. She stared at him, astonished. Then she drew herself up to her full height. "I've changed."

He blinked. "You? No, you haven't. Well, you're a little

older and prettier than ever. But you really haven't changed.''

"Oh, yes I have, Gus."

He started to shake his head in denial when she unfolded her arms and let her robe fall open.

His gaze traveled south. He stared at her belly.

The color drained from his face. He stumbled backward out onto the porch. "Mary? You're *pregnant?*"

She smiled beatifically and shut the door in his face.

Three

Pregnant?

Mary was *pregnant?*

Gus stood stock still on her doorstep, his mind the only thing moving. It reeled. He raised his hand to pound on the door again, then dropped it.

If he knocked and she opened it again, what could he possibly say?

There were no words.

She *couldn't* be pregnant! Not Mary! Not *his* Mary!

It meant she had another man.

He felt like he'd been kicked in the gut.

You expected maybe she was waiting for you? he asked himself savagely.

Well, now that you mentioned it… He was ashamed to admit that, yes, somehow he had expected that.

After all, she'd loved him! He'd loved her!

You left her, he reminded himself.

But…but…but…

He fumed. He scowled. He glared.

Finally he stomped off, jumped back into his truck and spun out, kicking up gravel as he roared away.

He needed to think. He tried. But thinking had never been high on Gus's list of accomplishments. It wasn't that he was stupid—at least he didn't think so most of the time—it was that he usually just went with his instincts. They'd served him well, for the most part.

But his instinct right now was to go bust open Mary's door and punch the lights out of whoever was the father of her child.

Fortunately he thought better of it.

As he drove, his mind grappled with the notion of Mary being someone else's woman. The old instincts were right on hand ready to reject it. But it wasn't easy—there was, after all, the memory of her very obviously pregnant belly.

It blew his mind.

It was the last thing he expected.

Just this afternoon his worst nightmare had been Mary having been pregnant with *his* child!

Now he had a worse one—Mary being pregnant now with someone else's!

Whose?

His fingers strangled the steering wheel. He glared into the oncoming headlights. A semi rumbled past. Gus felt as if it had just run him down.

He tried again to think. Becky had called her Miz McLean. So she *wasn't* married! He had half a second's relief before he remembered that a lot of women kept their maiden names these days. She could be married and be Miz McLean.

Had she been wearing a ring?

He hadn't been looking at her hands.

It didn't matter anyway. He knew Mary. She wouldn't be pregnant if she wasn't married. It was unthinkable. Impossible.

But Mary had scruples. She had values. She'd refused to make love with him until she was convinced they really loved each other, until she was sure they were going to be married and together forever.

It made him uncomfortable even now to remember that.

But it wasn't as if he'd duped her, he reminded himself. When they'd made love, he'd intended to marry her. He'd thought he was going to. He hadn't been feeling strangled in those days. That had come later.

Who was it?

Maybe Taggart knew. Or Felicity.

He'd ask as soon as he got back. Hell, maybe he knew the guy himself. An awful thought.

He tried to think of any guy he knew who might be worthy of Mary. He couldn't come up with one.

He got back to the ranch just in time to see the lights wink off at Taggart's house. Hell! Now he'd have to wait until morning.

One of the things Gus always told the wannabe bronc riders was to "be in the here and now."

When you were riding a bronc, he said bluntly, that wasn't the time to pick your nose. Or think about the fight you had with your wife. Or figure out whether you were going to the movies. Or decide what to have for dinner.

To ride broncs a guy had to focus, stay in the moment, pay attention.

And then he proved it. He went out and promptly got bucked off and stepped on by a horse he could have ridden when he was seven—and should have ridden today.

He would have ridden him just fine, thank you very much, if he hadn't been thinking about Mary.

"You okay?" Taggart, who was acting as pickup man, rode up alongside him.

Gus snagged his hat out of the dirt and slapped it against his thigh as he hobbled toward the fence. His ankle hurt like Hades where the bronc had stomped him. "Just dandy," he muttered. "Swell."

Taggart grinned. "Always instructive, taking a dive like that," he said cheerfully. "Makes 'em realize that not even the best of us has it licked."

Like he'd done it on purpose. Gus grunted.

"What do you know about Mary McLean?" he asked.

"Who?"

"Your daughter's teacher!" Gus glowered up at him. "What kind of a concerned parent are you?"

"A pretty damn good one most of the time," Taggart said, affronted. Then he grinned. "What about Mary?"

"Who's she married to?"

Taggart's brows lifted at Gus's harsh tone. "Who wants to know?"

"I do, damn it!" Gus drew a careful breath and did his best to sound rational. "We go back a long way, me an' Mary. I hadn't seen her in a while. I saw her yesterday when I picked Beck' up. An' she's pregnant!" He stopped because he knew he was sounding indignant. "I just wondered who her husband was. Anybody I know?"

"Doubt it," Taggart said. "She's not married."

"*What?*"

"She's not married," Taggart repeated.

"She's expectin' a baby!" Gus shouted.

"Mmm. Tell the world while you're at it," Taggart said mildly, looking around at a dozen pairs of interested eyes. All the cowboys in the place were staring at them.

"I don't have to tell anybody," Gus muttered. "You can damned well see it." He leveled an accusing glare on Taggart. "She's not married an' you're lettin' her teach in your schools?"

A slow grin spread across Taggart's face. One brow lifted. "Gettin' just a little prudish, are we, now?"

Gus ground his teeth. "I'm not a prude. I'm just… wonderin'. Beck' said she was new here. Reckoned you guys would've had to hire her when she was pregnant, and I just sorta thought the Elmer school board might be worryin' about what sort of example she would be settin' for your students if she didn't have a husband."

"Yeah, well, as I recall it was discussed," Taggart said. He turned his attention to the next bronc rider who was getting ready to go. "Felicity's on the board."

"So she hired her."

"She thought it would be a good idea to hire her."

"Even though she's an unwed mother."

"Hell, Gus, you really do have an ax to grind, don't you?"

"I just want to know why!"

"Ask her."

"Felicity?"

"No. Mary."

He didn't want to do that.

Gus was off to her right, somewhere behind her shoulder. Mary knew it without even having to turn around.

It was as if the air had changed the moment he'd come into the classroom. She'd had half a dozen students come in this afternoon to run through their speeches again. Becky had been one of them, and Mary had made her go first so she'd be ready to leave by the time her ride came—in case her ride was Gus.

It worked.

Becky was ready. But she didn't go.

Just as she'd finished, Mary had felt a well-remembered prickle of awareness on the back of her neck. Becky had smiled at someone in the back of the room. She'd started to pick up her things.

Then she'd stopped, looked quizzical, frowned slightly and had settled back into her chair with a shrug.

Mary frowned, too.

Why weren't they leaving? Then she thought maybe Gus had just come to tell Becky he had some errands to run and he'd be back. She took a deep breath, steadied herself and waited for the prickle to go away.

It never did.

He was there. Just behind her shoulder. Just beyond the corner of her eye.

And she couldn't concentrate on anything—but him! Her shoulders felt warm, as if touched by his breath. Hot—the way her mouth had been last night when he'd kissed her.

Which was the last thing she wanted to think about now!

She'd thought about it way too much already.

She'd scrubbed her face thoroughly—two or three times!—before she'd gone to bed last night. But if the taste of Gus was gone, the impression was still there. Even now she could feel his lips on hers.

She lifted a hand to touch her mouth, as if she needed to be sure they weren't still locked at the lips! Then she jerked her hand right back down again, furious at herself.

She knew he'd be watching—and remembering—and she wouldn't give him the satisfaction.

Suddenly she was aware of dead silence in the room. And was somehow equally aware that it had been going on a long time.

Sam Bacon stood at the podium, looking at her, waiting for her comments—and she didn't have a clue what to say.

She hadn't listened. And even if she had, she wouldn't have been able to say a word. Her tongue felt welded to the roof of her mouth. She cleared her throat, did her best to dredge up some saliva. She rubbed her palms briskly on the folds of her dress.

"Very well done," she said firmly. "Very strong delivery, Sam. Excellent!"

He looked startled at the praise. "You think it's better, me leavin' that whole section on Indian wood carving out accidentally?"

Had he? Oh, Lord.

"Well," Mary waffled, "you certainly, um, cut to the chase this time. Let me…think about it." Behind her she heard Gus snicker. She turned and shot him a quick, hard glare.

He grinned unrepentantly. Cheerfully. And then, damned if he didn't wink at her. Like they were sharing a joke.

Mary didn't want to share a joke with him. She didn't want to share anything with him. She wanted him gone. Determinedly she lumbered to her feet, intent on giving him a good eyeful of her burgeoning belly.

She wanted to remind him—wanted to make him think about her pregnant, about her with another man. She wanted him to go away and leave her alone!

But he just leaned against the doorjamb negligently, as if he had no intention of going anywhere.

"Becky is finished," Mary told him. "She can go."

"We'll listen," he said cheerfully and, whether Becky wanted to or not, they stayed.

Mary moved to the far side of the room and leaned against one of the bookcases. It wasn't as comfortable as sitting down, but it had the advantage of keeping her belly in plain view where Gus could see it every time he glanced her way.

But if it gave him a clear view of her, it gave her one of him, as well.

If she had changed, so had he. He was no longer the thin, wiry boy with the rust-colored hair and the quicksilver grin she remembered. Oh, the hair was still rust colored, what she could see peeking out from beneath his hat, and it wasn't even flecked with gray. The grin was even more lethal these days. But the boy's frame was gone now. Gus's shoulders were broader, his chest deeper. He was still lean and hard, though, with not a spare ounce of fat on him anywhere.

He still wore faded Wranglers and long-sleeved, muted-plaid shirts and his standard winter sheepskin jacket. His hat, too, was the same wool felt and, as always, black.

"Does that make you one of the bad guys?" she remembered asking him years ago.

He'd grinned and winked. "What do you think?"

At the time, fool that she was, she'd thought he was very good indeed.

Now she knew better.

Now she wished he'd just go away.

Mary had always been willowy. That had been her word for it at least.

"Bony," he used to call her back in high school, teasing her because he knew how much she envied her older sister, Ruthie's, curves.

"Willowy," Mary had insisted. "Svelte."

Then she'd thump him over the head with her history book or poke his ribs and say, "Talk about bony!" because in those days he'd been lanky, too.

She wasn't bony now. She looked like she had a beach

ball stuffed under her dress. But it wasn't a beach ball. It was a baby.

Some other guy's baby.

Some guy she wasn't married to.

Why?

Try as he might, Gus couldn't make sense of it.

And no amount of badgering had gotten an answer out of Taggart—or Felicity. He'd tried her, too.

But she'd said, "You ought to talk to Mary."

He'd muttered and grumbled, but his curiosity had been too great. He'd told Taggart he would pick Becky up after her speech practice. He'd come in and sat down, determined to wait, to ask.

It was true—it had to be—what Taggart and Felicity had said. Mary wasn't wearing a ring.

She'd worn his ring.

He remembered the day he'd slipped it on her finger. It had been, in his words, "the smallest diamond in Montana." But she'd been thrilled, and she'd thrown her arms around him and kissed him.

And she'd loved him—loved him with the sweet desperate innocence of youth.

She'd given *him* the gift of her virginity.

She'd been eighteen, he'd been nineteen. It had been both scary and beautiful. Neither of them had known what they were doing.

Mary wasn't supposed to know, of course. And Gus had figured anything that basic ought to be instinct.

He hadn't known much about giving and taking in those days. It had been quick—way too quick—and kind of messy when at last he and Mary had fumbled through it together. He had taken way more than he had given.

And it had been beautiful.

She had been beautiful, lying there on that blanket in the meadow, looking up at him, kissing him, touching him.

He groaned now.

The girl giving her speech at the front of the room stopped abruptly and looked straight at him.

Gus turned bright red.

"What's the matter?" Becky hissed in his ear.

Mortified, he shook his head. "Sorry," he muttered to the girl whose speech he'd interrupted. "I was…distracted."

He didn't look at Mary. Couldn't. His face was burning.

"We should go," Becky said out of the corner of her mouth.

But Gus wasn't leaving. Not until he'd talked to Mary. Resolutely he shook his head.

"Why not?"

But Gus didn't answer. He sat up straight, adjusted his jeans, which had become embarrassingly snug—cripes, it was exactly like being back in high school again!—and forced himself to pay attention. To act like an adult. To get a grip.

The girl finished, then Mary critiqued her speech. Her words were thoughtful and measured. Clearly she wasn't having problems concentrating.

Gus hoped the girl would be the last speaker. But no, a lean, wiry boy headed to the podium next. Gus sighed.

First the boy dropped his notes, then he dropped his pencil. Then he banged his head against the podium. Gus swallowed his snicker this time.

Mary was determinedly smiling and nodding at the boy, telling the kid to take his time, to breathe deeply and compose himself, then to start when he was ready.

Just do it and get it over with, Gus would have told him.

Patience had never been Gus's long suit.

As if the kid realized it, he looked at Gus, then gulped, then hiccupped. His face went bright red.

"It's all right, Race," Mary said. "Just begin."

"But he's—"

"He's listening," Mary said through her teeth.

The kid sighed, then began. After the first sentence was out, Gus was astonished to discover that the boy was actually damn good. And he was talking about bronc riding, of all things, just the way Gus had said he'd like to do.

Shooting periodic nervous glances in Gus's direction, the boy explained what went into a ride—how he prepared mentally and physically—and Gus sat there, nodding his head, understanding and agreeing.

The kid glanced up, saw him nod and turned even redder. He talked faster, his hands jammed into his pockets, finished in a rush, then didn't even wait for Mary's comments, but grabbed his notes and bolted back to his desk and sat down.

Mary took a deep breath. "Very well done, Race. There's lots of good information there. I know it's a little nerve-racking giving a talk on a subject with an expert in the audience, but I think you did really well, considering."

Gus looked around for the expert, and suddenly realized they were all looking at him!

He shook his head quickly. "Not me!"

He was used to being recognized on the rodeo circuit. He liked it there, thrived on it. But here it made him feel awkward. Especially when Mary looked at him, too, expectantly, as if he should be making intelligent comments.

She turned to her students. "For those of you who don't know him, Gus Holt is one of the premier bronc riders in America today. And from his reaction to your speech, Race, I'd say he thinks you did a pretty fine job. Do you have any suggestions, Mr. Holt?"

Mr. Holt?

Nobody called Gus *Mr. Holt.*

"That's my father," he said, then felt dumber than ever—and put on the spot—the way he often had when called on in school. And Mary, damn it all, knew it!

"He did good. You did real good," he said directly to the boy, who blushed to the roots of his hair. "You were right, too," he went on, Taggart having taught him that specifics were important when you were trying to get something across. "It is mostly mental preparation. But then you just gotta get out there and do it."

Like now, he thought, took a single desperate gulp of air and looked square at Mary.

"Have dinner with me tonight," he blurted.

You could have heard the chalk dust settle. The entire room went absolutely still. The students, all of them from Race to Becky, stared first at him and then—as if they were watching a tennis match and the ball had been smacked into the other court—their heads swiveled as one to stare at Mary.

She looked dumbfounded—and as uncomfortable as he had felt when she'd put him on the spot a minute before.

Her face was red, too, Gus was pleased to see. And she was opening and closing her mouth like a fish.

Then, "Thank you," she said politely. "But, no."

He gaped at her.

She had already turned her attention to another student. "All right, Tom. You're next. The rest of you don't need to hang around," she said to the group at large, but she wasn't talking to them, and both she and Gus knew it. Her words were aimed at him.

But he wasn't going anywhere. No sir. Everyone else got up and, gathering their things, began to head for the door—including Becky.

"Let's go," she said.

He didn't move. He continued to stand there, his fingers balled in frustration.

"Gus?" Becky said impatiently.

But he didn't even glance her way. He kept his gaze on Mary who would not look at him. It was like she was afraid of him. The thought startled him.

She couldn't be! When had he ever done anything to—

He didn't even have to finish the sentence. To hurt her? He began to understand for the first time just how badly he probably had.

Bad enough that things had changed—and not just because she was pregnant. Bad enough that she didn't even want to talk to him.

The room was silent.

Becky waited.

The boy, Tom, was at the podium, looking nervously at Mary, then at him.

Gus jammed his hands into his pockets. He sighed, then slanted Mary a glance. "Right," he muttered. "Sorry." Then he turned and followed Becky.

Mary's voice stopped him at the door. "Gus."

He spun back. "What?"

She was pale as she ran her tongue over her lips. She swallowed. "Come by at eight."

She was clearly out of her mind.

Why else, Mary asked herself as she paced around her living room, would she have done anything so stupid as to invite Gus over this evening?

It wasn't as if she wanted to see him!

In fact she *didn't* want to see him!

But if she didn't face him, she knew he'd think she was afraid to, that he'd think she hadn't ever gotten over him.

And she had, damn it!

She was over him. Completely.

More or less.

Facing him, she would get over him, Mary assured herself. She would tell him about the baby, inquire politely into the past dozen years of his life—and then she would say good-night. He would leave—and that would be that.

She just wished her heart didn't still kick over in her chest every time she thought about him. It would be so much easier if she could be indifferent to him.

She sighed. She didn't think she'd be indifferent to Gus even when she was dead.

The old oak mantel clock chimed eight times. As it finished, there was a knock on the door.

Even though she'd told him to come by at eight, the sound startled her.

She'd been glancing out the window every few minutes, looking for his truck, listening for the sound of an engine. But she'd never seen headlights. She hadn't heard a thing.

Maybe it wasn't Gus, she thought with a spurt of hope. Maybe it was Alice or Cloris dropping by to visit. She opened the door.

It was Gus.

She frowned.

"You said eight," he reminded her.

"I didn't hear your truck. I didn't see..." She stopped. She wasn't going to tell him she'd been watching out the window.

"You didn't see me pacing around out there?" A grin tugged at the corner of his mouth. "I saw you."

Her face flamed at the knowledge that he'd seen her peeking through the curtains. "What do you mean, pacing out there? Where were you?"

"I parked down by the Dew Drop. Got a little fortification—" his mouth twisted wryly "—and walked up from there."

"Fortification?" Mary said warily. She'd seen Gus "fortified" in the past.

"One beer," he assured her. "For courage."

"What do you need courage for?"

He looked so pointedly at her belly that she flushed and wrapped her arms across it. "This has nothing to do with you," she told him.

He didn't respond to that, just waited. "Are we going out or am I coming in?"

"Out?"

"I invited you to dinner," he reminded her.

"And I declined. I've eaten. Haven't you?"

"Nope. You could feed me." He gave her a patented Gus Holt grin, equal parts charming and hopeful.

"Some things never change," she muttered.

"And, as you pointed out," he said, looking at her belly, "some things do." He lifted his gaze and it locked with hers.

Mary sighed. "Come on in."

Gus had always reckoned he'd be willing to follow Mary's curves pretty much anywhere. Now, as he followed her through the living room and dining room he saw no reason to change his opinion. She still had the nicest looking rear end he could remember. Once upon a time he'd been in the habit of coming up behind her and dragging her back against him, fitting her bottom snug against him. He remembered how well she'd fit, how good it felt, how—

Not a good thing to be thinking about right now!

Not if he wanted to keep his cool.

He cleared his throat and glanced around for something to distract him from the physical Mary McLean. So he studied her house, looking for signs of the man who had got her in the family way.

He couldn't see anything that made him think the jerk

was living with her. Granted the furniture wasn't the cute feminine stuff he sometimes saw in the apartments of women he met, but even though it was heavy oak stuff in mission style—and not reproduction, either, from the look of it—there was nothing else in the room that made it look as if a guy was living with her. No boots by the door. No hunting magazines on the coffee table. No old socks or rodeo programs or beer bottles.

The room was small and cozy and neat, with light peach-colored walls and dark woodwork, built-in oak bookcases, Charlie Russell paintings and a worn oriental rug that looked as though it had been here since the house had been built some eighty years before. It all looked real homey, comfortable. Permanent.

Yet according to Taggart and Felicity, Mary had only been here since summer.

He tried to figure it out. Couldn't.

"I like your place," he said finally. That was true.

"So do I. There aren't a lot of rental properties in a town the size of Elmer. I was lucky. The principal knew about it because one of her former teachers owns it. Felicity Jones."

"Felicity owns this place?" Gus couldn't keep the surprise out of his voice. Well, hell, no wonder she knew about Mary. And why the hell hadn't she said? Why hadn't Taggart said?

"She inherited it from her uncle," Mary went on. "She lived here when she first came to town and was happy to rent it to another teacher when I came. Would you like another beer? More courage?" She raised one brow as she looked at him speculatively.

Gus nodded absently. He probably should have said no. It might be smarter to keep his wits about him. But when Mary turned and opened the refrigerator, then bent to take out a bottle, he decided he'd made the right decision after all.

Mary bending over to snag a beer gave him an even better view than just walking behind her had. Way too soon she straightened up and turned to hand him the bottle.

"Thanks." He opened it and lifted it to his lips when he realized she had only got out one. "You're not having any?" He frowned. Mary had never drunk much, but she hadn't been a teetotaler, either.

"I don't drink. Not now," she explained and laid a hand on her belly as if that was explanation enough.

As far as Gus was concerned, it just posed more questions. How the hell could she be careful with her kid and mislay its father?

Or had the bastard run out on her?

"Where is he?"

Mary had gone back to the refrigerator to take out containers, but at the harshness of his tone, she looked over her shoulder. "He who?"

He jerked his head in the direction of her midsection. "The father." He almost spat the words. "Did he dump you? He's not livin' here."

She set the containers on the counter, then shut the door before she turned to face him. "No." Her tone was even, casual, indifferent almost. "He's not."

"So where is he? You're not married to him."

She blinked. "How do you know?"

"Taggart told me. But I would've known anyhow. You're not wearin' a ring. Why didn't he marry you?"

"He's married to someone else."

It was the last thing on earth he expected her to say. *"What!"*

She dumped the contents of one of the containers into a saucepan. "This is green chile stew. Is it okay if I reheat it for you?"

"Whatever." It could have been barbed wire and jingle-bobs for all he cared. How could she talk about food when she'd just told him she'd been sleeping with a married man? "What do you mean, he's married?"

"He's married," she said. "You know, when two people go before a minister or justice of the peace and vow to love and honor and cherish each other for the rest of their natural lives?" She gave him a tight smile.

"Then why the hell was he sleepin' with you!"

She set the spoon on the counter and turned to face him, her arms wrapped across her belly. "Why the hell," she asked quietly, "should I answer that?"

Their gazes locked, hers as blue and frank and guileless as Gus could ever remember. She was Mary. Sweet, pure, innocent Mary.

Mary wouldn't have an affair. Not the Mary he knew.

But she was pregnant.

He shook his head, confused. He couldn't answer her. But knowing her the way he had, he couldn't make sense of the evidence before his eyes. At the same time Gus knew he had no right to ask for an explanation at all.

He'd walked out of her life years ago. He'd given up his claim. And yet...

He took off his hat, raked his fingers through his hair, then jammed it back down again. "It don't make sense," he muttered. "You wouldn't do that." Then he turned to go. "Never mind. I shouldn't have asked." He started for the door.

"Gus."

He looked over his shoulder.

Mary was smiling at him, a little sadly, a little wistfully, it seemed to him. "Thanks," she said.

"Huh?"

"Come on and sit down. I'll fix you dinner. And explain."

Four

She didn't begin, though, until she had his dinner on the table in front of him. While Mary sliced bread and put together some cottage cheese and pineapple for a salad, she tried to compose what she would say.

Of course she didn't have to give him any kind of explanation. She hadn't really intended to.

But because he'd believed in her—even despite the evidence and her own words—she found that she wanted to. She could see him simmering with impatience as he paced around the small kitchen.

She knew he wanted answers now. Gus always did. He always wanted everything now. But sometimes, she knew, he could wait.

If he had to. If he thought it was worthwhile.

Now he didn't press her.

"I can fix you a vegetable," she offered. "I have frozen peas and green beans."

"No. Thanks," he added after a moment. He didn't sit down even though she'd set a place for him at the table.

"How about coffee? All I have is decaf. Or would you prefer another beer?"

"Coffee's fine." He tapped his toes and jammed his fingers into the pockets of his jeans, then just as quick, yanked them out again and cracked his knuckles. He took off his hat, rubbed a hand over his hair, then put the hat back on again, then apparently remembered where he was and took it off again and hung it on the hook by the door.

Even then he didn't sit. He tucked his fingers into his pockets, then bounced on his heels and then on his toes.

Mary dished up the stew and set it on the table, then pointed at the chair.

Gus sat. He didn't eat. He waited, watching like a panther as she poured them each a cup of coffee and finally, when she could think of no other way to stall and avoid the inevitable, came and sat down opposite him.

"Eat," she commanded, "before it gets cold."

He picked up his fork, then met her gaze. He nodded. He waited. It was her show, he seemed to be saying. "I'll eat. You talk."

"I'm wondering where to start."

"Whose kid is it?"

Her mouth twisted. Trust Gus to come right to the point. "My brother-in-law's."

His fork clattered to the table. *"What!"*

"*And* my sister's," Mary went on firmly. "You remember Ruthie."

He stared at her, poleaxed, then shook his head.

"It's Jeff and Ruthie's baby," Mary told him.

"I know I didn't do that great in biology, but—" Gus gave his head another shake "—I don't think I was that bad at it."

She smiled wryly. "You were always very good in biology, Gus. This is not…regular biology. It's the high-tech stuff. I'm not the mother. I'm the surrogate. I'm just… carrying their child."

He stared at her, looking a little dazed, a lot disbelieving and still considerably confused.

"Ruthie and Jeff have been married a dozen years. They have been trying to have a baby for almost as long. Ruthie's had seven miscarriages. She can get pregnant, but she can't carry a baby to term. Something to do with her uterus."

Ruthie could explain in precise medical terms exactly what was wrong, but knowing hadn't helped her carry a child. Nothing she or her doctors had done had been able to correct the problem.

"There was no way, given her condition, that she could carry a baby long enough for it to survive. The doctors finally told her that the only way to have one that was theirs biologically was to have some other woman carry it. So—" she shrugged "—I volunteered."

"To carry *her* baby?" Gus's words were barely audible.

Mary nodded. "The doctors fertilized one of Ruthie's eggs with Jeff's sperm, and I'm carrying it." She smiled. "I'm the incubator, that's all."

"All?" Gus looked dazed, the way he had when he'd ridden his father's new sorrel stallion and had landed on his head.

Mary reached out and pushed his cup of coffee at him. "It's not a big deal," she told him briskly. "It's just… Ruthie's my sister. She wants a child. She and Jeff *both* want a child. Desperately. And I was in a position to help."

She didn't tell him how much she had come to want to do this, too. How much she wanted to share in the miracle of birth—even to a child she knew she wouldn't be able to keep.

For several years after Gus had broken their engagement, Mary had been sure she would find another man, marry and have a family. But time had passed, and though she'd dated other men, somehow the right man had never come along.

She was almost thirty-one now—and no nearer the marriage and family she'd always dreamed of than when she'd first fallen in love with Gus. Farther from it, probably, because then she'd hoped.

Somehow over the past couple of years, her hopes had waned.

She'd dated plenty of men. And none of them had come close to sparking in her the same feelings, the same emotions, the same connection she'd once felt with Gus.

She began to think there never would be another man for her.

And if there wasn't a man, there wouldn't be children, either.

So, when Ruthie had tearfully told her the bad news, that she would never be able to carry a child to term, Mary had found herself saying, "I could do that."

"So this is not…your kid?" Gus's gaze flicked back and forth between her face and her abdomen.

"No." Even though Mary sometimes felt as if it were. She had to keep telling herself she was not really this baby's mother or she'd become far too attached, and she knew it.

"No," she said again. "It's Ruthie and Jeff's baby."

She made herself say it. She said it every chance she got.

"You're just…having it, and then you're giving it up?"

"Yes," Mary said firmly.

There was a long silence.

"So you're not…" He stopped. Swallowed. "There is

no other..." He stopped again. He gave a shudder, like a dog shaking off cold water, then began grinning like a fool.

"No other what?" Mary asked.

But he didn't answer. He laughed. It was an odd, breaking laugh. "Well, damn," he said. Then, "How about that?" He laughed again.

Mary watched warily. She didn't want Gus grinning like that.

It did disastrous things to her insides—especially to the inside of her brain. It made her remember happy times with him. Loving times.

"Eat your stew," she commanded gruffly.

Still grinning, Gus did.

She was his again!

His!

His?

Which meant what? Gus stopped shoveling in the stew and thought about that.

Discovering that not only wasn't there another guy in Mary's life, but that a man hadn't even been responsible for putting the child in her belly, made him euphoric.

Relieved beyond belief.

It was as if he'd been on a bronc, spinning out of control, and had suddenly found the rhythm. The world stopped reeling and came into focus. Life seemed right again.

Because Mary was in it.

He hadn't realized how much he'd missed sitting across the table from her, how much he liked looking up to find her there.

Which, again, meant what?

The *M* word nudged its way into his brain.

He resisted. He'd been resisting even thinking about marriage for years. The only person he'd ever considered marrying had been Mary. And once that had panicked him, he'd never thought about it again.

And now?

The word nudged its way back in again.

This time he wasn't so quick to push it back out. He let it sit there. He forked up a little stew and carried it to his mouth; all the while he mentally circled the word. *Marriage.*

Not right now, of course.

He didn't reckon Mary would have him right now. He had some pretty serious fence mending to do as far as Mary was concerned.

And he knew better than to make up his mind about something too quick. At least he thought he did.

But then he looked up and saw Mary sitting across the table from him, a cup of coffee in her hands, and he liked what he saw. He liked how it felt having her there. It didn't seem nearly as scary as it once had.

There had been plenty of years after he'd broken off their engagement when the very mention of the word *marriage* found him reaching to touch his neck to check for the noose.

If he hadn't been ready to marry Mary, he sure as heck hadn't been interested in a long-term commitment to any of several dozen other women who wanted to take him home to mother.

After so many years he hadn't really thought he'd ever be ready.

He'd expected to go through life on his own. Footloose and fancy-free.

Yet now, when he thought about it, being fancy-free wasn't all that appealing.

And he couldn't feel any noose around his neck. He could swallow his stew perfectly easily. He thought again about sitting down across from Mary not just tonight but during every mealtime. He didn't feel any panic at all.

In fact, it was downright appealing.

Maybe he was ready for marriage.

The sheer novelty of that notion choked him and made him start to cough.

Mary leaped up and slapped him on the back and got him a glass of water, then hovered over him while he gulped it down.

"Are you all right? Do you need more water? Can I get you anything?"

Still gasping, eyes watering, he sputtered and shook his head, then cleared his throat. "N-no. I'm...I'm fine. I...it just...I swallowed wrong."

He shot her a quick glance, wondering what she'd say if he told her. His life was worth more than that!

No, he would have to take it slow and easy around Mary. He'd have to gentle her the way J.D. gentled a skittish horse.

He couldn't expect her to welcome him back with open arms.

But he wanted to come back. He wanted to find out if his panic was truly gone. He wanted to be part of her life again. He wanted her to be part of his.

"Do you need more water, Gus?" She was still hovering, still looking down at him worriedly. "What do you need?"

It was an impulse, pure and simple. But he was on eye level with her burgeoning belly, and he said simply, "This," and he leaned forward and planted a kiss right on it.

Mary jumped a foot.

Then she scrambled away to the other side of the table,

where she stood hanging on to the back of her chair, keeping both it and the table between them.

"What do you think you're doing?" she demanded. Her cheeks were scarlet, her eyes like saucers as she glared at him.

He slanted a grin up at her. "Just sayin' hi."

"Well, it's not necessary!" Her knuckles were white on the chair back, and it looked like she was trembling. He figured it was probably the shock and not that she was displeased.

He shrugged amiably. "I just wanted you to know I'm happy for you—for him...or her—and for Ruthie and Jeff."

"Well, um, thank you." Mary still looked flustered. She still stayed away across the room from him.

"Hey, I used to kiss you there, Mar'," Gus said gently.

Mary's cheeks grew even redder, and she wrapped her arms across her body as if she were huddling behind them. "That was a long time ago."

Gus nodded gravely. "Too long."

"Not nearly long enough." Then she gave herself a little shake and said, "I think you'd better go, Gus."

"Aw, Mary. I wasn't tryin' to rile you. I just wanted you—and that baby—to know I was pleased."

"I think you better go."

She looked upset. He didn't want her upset. He didn't figure it was good for pregnant women to be upset. So he nodded and shoved away from the table and stood up. When he did so, Mary backed up even farther.

He frowned. "I'm not gonna hurt you," he told her, because for some crazy reason she was acting as if she was scared of him.

She kept her arms wrapped across her belly. "No," she said with obvious determination. "You're not."

Like it was a vow or something. He snagged his hat and set it on his head, then shrugged into his jacket. "It was real good stew, Mary. Thanks."

"You're welcome." She didn't budge from behind the chair.

He looked at her for a long moment. She was even prettier than he remembered. Vital. Vibrant. Pregnancy agreed with her. He imagined her big with *his* child—and the thought, far from making him panic, brought a grin to his face.

"You look beautiful," he told her.

She glared at him. "Go away, Gus."

He kept on grinning, even as he nodded and headed for the door. "I'm goin'," he assured her.

But I'll be back, he thought to himself as the door closed behind him.

Because he wasn't drifting now. He wasn't aimless any longer. He had a goal again.

Mary.

Damn him.

Damn, damn, damn him. That was all Mary could think as she tossed and turned in bed that night. Usually the baby's kicks kept her awake, but the baby was uncommonly subdued this evening. Or maybe Mary just didn't notice any other agitation because her own was so great.

She'd tried to grade papers after Gus left. But she couldn't concentrate. Then she'd tried watching a movie on television. But it couldn't keep her attention. She kept rubbing her belly, distracted, kept thinking that something was touching it.

But nothing was touching it—except the memory of Gus's lips.

How could he do something like that?

How could he kiss her—*there*—of all places?

Most men she knew took one look at her expansive midriff and backed away, as if they thought her pregnancy might rub off and make them fathers.

Single men were particularly susceptible. But even the happily married men she knew—Felicity's husband for example—tended to give her wide berth because, as Taggart said, ''There've been enough babies at the Jones house.''

But Gus hadn't backed off.

He'd leaned forward—and kissed her belly!

The intimacy of it shocked her. And no matter how she tried to blot it out, she could feel it still. It unnerved her more than the kiss he'd given her yesterday. That one was easily rationalized as Gus behaving like Gus. This…this wasn't Gus at all.

The gentle press of his lips against her abdomen was a sensation that should have vanished hours ago. It hadn't.

Nor had the memory of his lopsided grin and the sparkle in his deep-green eyes. She didn't want to think about them—about him!—but she couldn't seem to stop.

No man had ever tempted her the way Gus had.

No man had hurt her like Gus.

She dragged the pillow over her face and shut her eyes as if that would help. In a dozen years she hadn't been able to blot out the memory of Gus Holt.

Why should she be able to tonight?

It was a relief when the phone rang, even though it was past midnight. She snatched it up. ''Hello?''

''Hi.'' It was Ruthie sounding breathless. ''Are you all right?''

Mary took a deep breath. ''Of course. I'm fine. Why wouldn't I be?'' She'd been reassuring Ruthie for the past six months—ever since they'd found out for sure that the pregnancy was proceeding.

"I've been getting vibes," her sister said.

"Well, you'd better stop getting them," Mary replied firmly. "Everything's fine."

It was uncanny, really, how her sister seemed so attuned to things going on in Mary's body even though Ruthie was a thousand miles away. But early on she had somehow sensed those days when Mary had been most nauseated with morning sickness. And she had called, flustered and convinced something momentous had happened the night Mary had felt the first faint flutterings of the baby kicking in her womb.

"How did you know?" Mary had demanded then.

"I'm the mother," Ruthie had replied. "I *know*."

Now Ruthie demanded, "Are you sure? I feel something. Nothing's happening?"

"Nothing," Mary said. "Except…Gus is here."

Why she said it, she didn't know.

Maybe she just needed to talk to someone. And Ruthie had been so supportive the first time. Ruthie had been the rock Mary had leaned on, the one who had assured her there was nothing wrong with her, that she had nothing to be ashamed of when she'd had to call off the wedding. She'd even come up from Arizona to be there with her. She was the one who had talked Mary into leaving Montana and moving down to live with her and Jeff to attend school at Arizona State.

"*Gus! Gus Holt?* That jerk?"

"He's not exactly a jerk."

"Don't defend him!" Ruthie said hotly. "He jilted you. He left you at the altar. He got cold feet and ran off!"

"He didn't jilt me," Mary corrected. "And he didn't leave me at the altar. He called a week ahead of time."

"To tell you he had cold feet and couldn't go through with it."

"Yes, but—"

"It amounts to the same thing," Ruthie said firmly. "I remember how hurt you were. You were a wreck. I don't want him hurting you again."

"He won't." Mary was sure about that. She wouldn't let him. "He's just passing through."

"As fast as he can, no doubt."

"Probably," Mary agreed. She hoped so, anyway. He'd been around far too long already for her peace of mind.

She wished she'd asked him how long he would be here, but she hadn't wanted to act as if she cared. She *didn't* care, she reminded herself. She only cared that soon he would be gone!

"How's our guy?" Ruthie asked, changing the subject and the tone of her voice. It softened every time she mentioned the baby. There was a wistful, gentle ache in the mere sound of it. "Did he have a good day?"

"Yes," Mary said. *Gus kissed him.* She didn't say that. "He's doing very well."

"And you are, too?" There was always a thread of apprehension in Ruthie's tone when she asked that question, as if something might happen. "You don't have to stay up there, you know," Ruthie said for the umpteenth time. "Montana is a long way away. You ought to come home." Ruthie hadn't totally given up trying to persuade Mary to come back to Arizona. "You wouldn't have to teach. You could just rest," she said now. "You need your rest."

"I need to keep busy, too," Mary replied and went on to talk about the kids and their speeches. She talked at such length that Ruthie was finally the one to end the conversation.

"You need your sleep," she said at last. "It must be later there. I'll talk to you on Sunday."

"Yes," Mary agreed. She hung up, too. And lay there

in the dark, staring at the ceiling, trying to think about the speech contest. The baby kicked—just about where Gus had kissed her.

She rubbed her belly.

Gus had never been to a junior high speech contest in his entire life.

If you'd asked him a week ago if he ever thought he'd go to one, he would have given you a one-word answer— and it wouldn't have been yes.

But when Becky asked if he'd like to come watch her give her speech on Saturday, he surprised her and her parents and even himself by jumping at the chance.

"You mean it?" Becky goggled at him. She gulped hard and, he thought, looked a little sick.

"Yeah, I'd like to," he said. "Noah said he didn't need me on Saturday, so why not?"

Why not, indeed? He'd get to spend the entire day watching Mary.

He'd watched Mary every afternoon for the rest of the week. He'd made it a point to be the one who went in to pick Becky up at school. And he'd always managed to get there early so he could sit in the back and listen. And watch Mary.

He'd tried doing more. He'd called her the day after she'd told him about the baby. He'd asked if she wanted to go out to eat.

No, thank you, she'd said.

Did she want to catch a movie in Bozeman, then?

No, thank you. Again.

Did she want to come have dinner at Jones's? Felicity had said to invite her.

No, thank you very much.

She was busy Wednesday. Thursday. Friday. She was busy whatever night he asked.

She didn't want to go out with him. She finally told him that point-blank last night when he'd called.

"You don't like me?" he'd asked. "You used to like me. You used to love me."

"That was then," she'd said. "And it was a long time ago."

"Yeah, it was. We were kids. We're grown-ups now. You could give me another chance."

"No," she'd said. "Goodbye, Gus. Don't call me again."

He supposed he couldn't really blame her. He'd hurt her.

But he wouldn't hurt her this time, damn it! It didn't seem entirely fair to hold his nineteen-year-old self's stupidity against his thirty-one-year-old self's hard-won maturity—such as it was—but he didn't think Mary would buy that.

So he figured he'd take it easy. Take it slow. Turn up where she was. Let her see he'd come a long way in a dozen years.

Having Becky invite him to the speech contest was like having a roast duck fall into his lap.

The day-long contest was being held in a small auditorium on the Montana State University campus. Mary was already there when they arrived. She was wearing a navy blue maternity jumper and a white blouse that had the effect, Gus thought, of making her look like a very pregnant very sexy nun. Her long golden hair was done up in some intricate knot at the back of her head. It looked neat and orderly and made Gus long to thread his fingers through it and mess it up.

She already had several of her students in a group at the front of the auditorium, and when she spotted Becky sh waved her over. Her hand stopped midwave when she spotted him.

Gus grinned, waggled his fingers in a little wave in her direction, then followed Taggart and Felicity to their seats.

He'd had a week now to watch the way Mary worked with her students in small groups as well as individually.

Today he saw the results she got. He was impressed.

She gave her students confidence in themselves. She showed them how to do a good job, then she got out of the way and let them do it.

The boy she'd called Race had come a long way. He might have been white-knuckling the podium through his whole speech, but it didn't slow him down any. And he never stood there, tongue-tied and helpless, the way Gus was sure he would have been.

The two seventh-grade girls were good, too. And so was the boy, Tom, who looked like a wrestler but talked about computer circuitry and telecommunications in the twenty-first century.

But Becky was the best. No doubt about it. He wasn't at all surprised when the winner in her category was announced and Becky won.

He was as proud as Taggart—and not just of Becky. Of Mary, too, who had taught her well.

That was what he told her afterward.

"You did good," he said as they were all milling around, parents and students and teachers, getting ready to leave.

"I didn't do anything," she said, struggling to pull on her coat.

Gus took it out of her hands and held it for her to slip on. She scowled at him. He just held it out and waited. When she still didn't move, he grinned at her and waved the coat a little. It was red. "I feel like a bullfighter."

Mary's lips twitched, and finally she laughed just a little.

She also slipped her arms into the sleeves of her coat. Gus settled it around her shoulders, taking way more time and care than he needed to. Her hair brushed his cheek. He could smell her shampoo—and a subtle smell he remembered as being just purely Mary.

It made his knees wobble.

"Ready for dinner?" Taggart said cheerfully with Willy on his shoulders as they headed for the parking lot. It was beginning to snow a little. "Let's all go celebrate. You, too, Ms. McLean."

"Oh, no. I don't want to butt in," Mary said quickly. "This is Becky's party."

"And Becky would be delighted to have you celebrate with us," Taggart said. "Wouldn't you?" He anchored Willy's feet with one hand and gave his older daughter a one-armed hug.

Eagerly Becky nodded. "Yes, please." She was grinning all over her face, had been since she'd finished her speech.

Gus would have said yes, please, too, but he figured that would just drive her in the other direction. As it happened there were enough other people to persuade her. Taggart's parents, who lived in Bozeman, had come for the contest, and they added their wish to have Mary join them. And when Felicity made her admit that she didn't have anywhere else to go, Mary had no choice but to agree to come along.

They went to a steak house west of town. It was a rambling low-slung building with dark wood paneling and an old-time western flavor. It wasn't yet crowded in the late afternoon, though Gus knew it would be jammed and rocking off its foundation later. He'd spent many a Saturday night there, flirting with the waitresses and local buckle bunnies and the occasional out-of-her-element college girl.

The waitress eyed him appreciatively this time, too, but

Gus wasn't interested in flirting. He was interested in Mary—and perfectly happy to be part of a family group.

He didn't have to work too hard to end up sitting next to her. Taggart got them a big round table where Gus wound up with Becky on one side of him and Mary on the other.

"The two prettiest girls in the room," he said in a voice loud enough so only they could hear.

Mary shot him a disapproving look, but Becky turned red. He reached out and tweaked her long braid. "You did great today."

She beamed. "Thanks."

He was careful to spend at least half the meal talking to her. It was enough, he assured himself, to have Mary next to him, to casually and accidentally let his knee nudge hers, to let his fingers brush hers when he asked her to pass him the cole slaw or the apple sauce.

They talked about Becky's speech, then Taggart told his own version of training Domino, which led to more stories from his dad about horses they had trained. That led, naturally enough, to Gus telling stories about horses his own trainer father, Dan, and J.D. had worked with.

"How is J.D.?" Mary asked.

It was the first real interest she'd shown. He took heart. "He's fine," Gus said heartily. "Gettin' married, would you believe? To Lydia Cochrane."

He could tell that surprised her as much as it had surprised him. Proper lawyer Lydia had never seemed the sort of woman who would want to take on a hardheaded son-of-a-gun like J.D.

"People change," he explained, meeting her gaze.

They looked at each other a long moment. She didn't reply.

Then Willy wanted to share his sandwich, and Abby offered him some French fries, and they never got back to the stuff that mattered.

Not until Mary suddenly lurched beside him, and Felicity laughed and said, "Baby kick you?"

And Mary flushed and nodded. She pressed a hand on her belly.

"Can I feel?" Willy's eyes were like saucers. And when he had, Abby needed to—and then Becky.

Gus wasn't about to be left out.

"I've never felt a baby kick," he said, and put his hand on her belly before she could stop him. Then the baby kicked, and Gus, not Mary, was the one who jerked.

"Holy cow!" he exclaimed, astonished.

And Mary laughed, then quickly looked away. But not before Gus had seen a flicker of warmth in her eyes. He was elated.

When they came out of the restaurant into a howling snowstorm, things got even better.

"You'd better take Gus with you," Taggart said to Mary as they were walking to their cars.

But she shook her head. "That's not necessary. I'll be fine."

Gus opened his mouth to argue with her, but he didn't have to. Taggart did it for him.

"Not in that, you won't," Taggart said. Her car was a late-model foreign import. Not like the full-size pickups and wagons everyone else drove.

Even Felicity shook her head. "You shouldn't be driving over the pass alone in bad weather. You said yourself you don't remember much about driving in snow."

Still Mary hesitated. "Well, I—"

"It's nothing to fool around with," Taggart said firmly. "I got hit a few years ago in a storm no worse than this one."

"He almost died," Becky told her with ghoulish good cheer.

Mary blanched.

"Don't take a risk, my dear," Taggart's mother said.

"Not when you can have Gus take you," his father added.

Mary gave Gus a hard look, one that accused him of having put them all up to this.

But for once Gus was entirely blameless. He grinned guilelessly. "If you'd rather I didn't..."

She ran her tongue over her lips, then pressed them shut in a firm line and shrugged reluctantly. "I guess you'd better," she muttered ungraciously. Then added with equal reluctance, "Thanks."

"Do you have a cell phone?" Felicity asked.

At Mary's nod, Taggart scribbled down a number and handed it to her. "That's ours. We'll drive ahead of you. You can watch the taillights," he said to Gus. "Call if you have problems."

"We won't have problems," Gus said firmly. He held out his hand for Mary's keys.

She looked at him once more a little nervously, then fished them out and handed them to him.

Smiling, Gus unlocked the door. Then, like the chivalrous gentleman his dear sainted dead mother would have been astonished to finally see, he opened it for her and waited while she settled herself inside.

"We'll be fine," he promised. "Piece of cake. Nothing to worry about."

Mary muttered something under her breath. It sounded like, "We'll see."

Five

"You don't have to do this," Mary said as he got in the driver's side.

"I want to."

She scowled. "I know."

Their eyes met again, and hers flashed with annoyance.

Gus just grinned. He settled in beside her, then reached over and took her gloved hand in his and squeezed it. "Trust me, Mar'. I'll get you home safe and sound."

She didn't look at him, just slid her fingers out of his and knotted them with her others on top of her blooming belly. It sobered him at once.

He realized all at once that this wasn't a game—and it wasn't just about him and Mary.

He had a baby to get home safe and sound, too.

He looked at where her hands lay protectively on her abdomen. "You're not...havin' it...or anything. Are you?"

She shot him a quick astonished glance. "What, now? No. Of course not. I'm not due for nearly three months."

"Oh." He took a deep breath. "That's all right then."

But he still used excruciating care as he eased her car back and drove slowly out of the parking lot. Taggart was already heading up the onramp onto the interstate.

Gus could just see his taillights ahead and he stepped on the gas a little harder in an effort to catch up.

If he'd thought that he'd charm her in their time together, he soon realized he couldn't. He had to concentrate on the road.

Gus had driven in his share of bad weather. He'd seen gully washers and tornadoes, blizzards and ice. He'd survived dust storms and flash floods and one Louisiana hurricane. He'd considered them a challenge. He'd relished the experience.

He wasn't relishing this.

What if something happened? To the car? To Mary? To the baby?

He wasn't used to having the responsibility for another person. It was sobering. Daunting.

"Trust me," he'd said blithely an hour before.

But he wondered more than once as they bounced and slid over the pass and down the other side, if she ought to be trusting him at all.

And by the time they finally turned off the highway into Elmer, Gus felt like he'd ridden a bucking bronc for eight hours, not eight seconds. And as they turned onto Apple Street, he took a deep, relieved breath.

One moment too soon.

The car hit an icy patch as he tried to stop. It skidded sideways and slid straight into Mary's front hedge.

"Cripes! You okay?" He almost didn't dare ask, afraid of what the answer might be.

But Mary gave a giddy laugh. "Wonderful!" And he looked over to see her smiling all over her face. "You did it! Thank you!" And she kissed him hard on the mouth!

It was the last thing he expected, nothing he'd dared hope for.

But before he could hope at all, she jerked back. Fast. "I'm sorry! I didn't mean—"

He grinned. "Don't apologize."

"I just…I was just…saying thank you. I was relieved, you know." She was backpedaling as fast as she could go.

"You can thank me anytime you want." He started to lean toward her again when suddenly the passenger door was wrenched open and Becky poked her head in.

"Everything okay? My dad wants to know if you're okay," she said to Mary.

The color still high in her cheeks, Mary twisted around toward Becky. "Yes. Yes, I'm fine. We were just…"

"Kissing," Gus said softly.

Mary shot him a glare. "I'm just getting out."

"You hit the hedge," Becky said to Gus. "Are you okay?"

"Fine." He was still smiling. He could still feel Mary's lips on his own. Then Taggart was there, helping Mary out of the car and saying to Gus, "What the hell were you thinking? You hit the hedge, for God's sake!"

Gus just grinned at him, too.

Mary got her briefcase out of the back seat and hugged it against her middle. "He did fine. He got me here," she said to Taggart, carefully not looking at Gus. "All safe and sound." She smiled at them all. "I'll just go in now. I just…" She still didn't look at Gus, not until the last moment. Then she darted a glance at him. "Thanks. Thanks to all of you." She headed for the house.

Gus went after her. "I've got your keys."

She held out her hand for them, but he shook his head, took the briefcase away from her and held out his arm.

She hesitated just a moment. But short of making a scene in front of Taggart and Becky, which he knew she wouldn't do, she had no choice. She took hold of his elbow and let him lead her up the steps and to her door.

"Thank you." She even sounded like a schoolmarm now. All frost and hairpins.

Gus grinned. He reached around her hand, outstretched for the keys, and opened the door for her. Then he set her briefcase inside. "There."

When he straightened up again, they were only inches apart. He could feel the warmth of her breath on his cheek. She was close enough to kiss.

"How 'bout it, Mary?" he whispered.

She didn't even pretend not to know what he meant. She gave a quick sharp shake of her head. "It was a mistake, Gus. I was overwhelmed with gratitude."

"Is that what you were?" He lifted a mocking eyebrow.

"Yes. It was a thank-you, Gus. Nothing more. And I am not going to do it again. You've been thanked. And Taggart's waiting."

"Let him wait."

"Gus!"

He tried desperately to think of a reason to get her to see him again. He couldn't waste this advantage. "You remember what I said about J.D. and Lydia gettin' married? Well, it's…gonna be next weekend. You wanta come?"

The minute he said it, he knew he'd not only wasted whatever advantage he'd gained, but he'd dug himself into a hole a hundred feet deep.

A wedding—*any* wedding—was the last place Mary would go with him! It would bring back too many memories of what they hadn't had together—of what he'd walked out on.

Gus shut his eyes and damned his feeble brain. He could have kicked himself from here to Murray.

"Forget I said that," he muttered.

When he opened them again, it was to see that her smile was a little strained. "Thank you, but I don't think so. Give J.D. my best."

"Yeah. I'll do that."

He turned away, then turned back. "I'm not just walkin' away, Mar'," he said determinedly. "Not now that I've found you again."

She opened her mouth, but he wasn't going to listen to her argue—not when she'd kissed him like that! He knew the difference between gratitude and what that had been.

"I'll be around," he said firmly.

"Gus, I don't want—"

"Yes, you do." He met her gaze squarely. "You still want me, Mary. You do. And I want you."

"Want has nothing to do with it!"

"What the hell's that supposed to mean?"

She shook her head fiercely. "Nothing. You wouldn't understand!"

"I'd try. Come on, Mary."

"No. Goodbye, Gus. Thank you and goodbye."

He just looked at her. "I'm not walkin', Mar'. You'll see. When you're ready to admit it, I'll be around."

When she was ready to admit it, he'd be around!

How dare he!!!

He'd be around! Talk about words that were both threat and promise. Mary was afraid to think which.

But truly, just as she'd told him, *want* had nothing to do with it.

She had *wanted* Gus years ago. In her heart she'd *wanted* him all the years he was gone. And yes, heaven help her—though she would never ever admit it to him!—she was willing to admit she *wanted* him still.

The trouble was, she didn't trust him a bit.

And *trust* was ultimately what it was all about.

Trust was what relationships depended on. Trust was what made them work. She'd seen that with her parents, with Ruthie and Jeff, with Taggart and Felicity.

And Mary was determined that if she gave her heart to a man again, she would give it to a man she could trust not to break it.

Gus had broken it once.

She did not trust Gus.

She also could not seem to stop thinking about him. All week long she thought about him. All week long she remembered Gus in the distant past and Gus of the Saturday night drive home.

She couldn't seem to forget.

It would have helped if she'd been able to actively resist him all the way home. She'd resisted his driving her—until she realized it would be safer for him to do so.

But even then she'd expected to have to resist him during the drive. But he'd been too busy driving to pay any attention to her. All his focus was on the road and the car.

That meant, unfortunately, that she'd been able to study him at length instead of ignoring his very presence.

At first she'd watched his profile surreptitiously. But once she realized he was too preoccupied with the storm to notice what she was doing, she'd stared at him openly and compared what she remembered of him as a boy with the man he had become.

She could still catch glimpses of that younger Gus in his profile. In his right cheek she could still see the crease that became a dimple when he grinned. Above his deep-set eyes there were still those impossibly long lashes that she used to tease him about. And his nose still sported a bump where, during his last year of high school, a fence had broken his fall from a bronc.

But he had changed, too.

Webs of fine lines radiated out from his eyes now. They were lines that told her Gus had seen more than thirty hard years of an eventful life. They said he'd squinted into his share of harsh sunlight and had laughed and enjoyed what life had brought his way.

Gus had always enjoyed life. He'd made her enjoy life— had made her laugh, had teased and tickled her, had brought her whimsical gifts and told her crazy jokes. She'd missed the jokes, the teasing, the tickling—the boy.

How much of all that, she wondered, was still in the man?

He was still clean shaven. He'd never, as far as she knew, gone for the mustache that many rodeo cowboys wore. But the shadow of whiskers on his jaw was darker than she remembered. It was heavier, rougher, and she'd wondered how it would feel against her cheek, against her palm.

She'd knotted her fingers even more tightly, afraid that they might reach out and touch him—might decide of their own accord to find out what it felt like to touch Gus Holt again.

Determinedly she'd shut her eyes and looked away. But it wasn't long before she'd been looking at him again.

She'd found a small scar on the right side of his jaw that hadn't been there a dozen years ago. It was maybe an inch long, crescent shaped. A hoof? A horn? A broken bottle?

She'd had to bite her tongue not to ask him about it.

She wondered again now.

He hadn't come back since he'd brought her home that

night. But he hadn't left her alone, either—not really. He'd been in her thoughts and in her dreams all week long.

He might not have come by school. He might not have called. He might not have dropped by her house. But he didn't have to be there physically to be present.

He was driving her nuts.

It wouldn't last, she assured herself. Once he was gone, the memories would fade. And, despite what he said, she was sure Gus would go.

His ability to cool his heels in any given place had always rivaled the shelf life of a loaf of bread. His work with Taggart Jones and Noah Tanner was a casual thing. He wasn't moving in. He was hanging out.

This weekend, in fact, he'd be gone. He'd be heading up to Murray by Friday at least to attend his brother's wedding.

That ought to solve the problem right there. This was Gus, after all—a man allergic to marriage.

He'd doubtless take one look at his brother reciting vows that promised forever—a forever he'd chosen not to promise—and he'd keep right on going without once looking back.

Mary took heart from that.

Subtle was not a word in Gus's vocabulary.

He was a here-and-now man, a what-you-see-is-what-you-get, no-nonsense kind of guy. He flirted and teased, but he didn't play games.

He'd said what he meant to Mary last Saturday.

He meant what he'd said. He wanted her. She wanted him.

So why didn't she come to her senses and admit he was right?

He hadn't expected her to call the next day. She had a

right to make him sweat a little. He hadn't handled the breaking of their engagement well, and they'd been apart a long time.

He'd been willing to concede a day—or even two—so she could come to terms with the fact that he wasn't nineteen any more. He was grown-up now. And still interested in her.

Very interested.

But Monday came and went and so did Tuesday.

He wanted Mary to make a move.

She didn't make one on Wednesday. On Thursday he began to realize she wasn't going to.

She was going to pretend she didn't care.

How juvenile was that?

It would serve her right if he went to J.D.'s wedding and kept right on going. But when Becky asked him, after dinner Thursday night when he was throwing his gear into his truck so he could make an early start tomorrow, if he was coming back, he'd said, "You bet I'm coming back."

And he'd been pleased to see Becky beam. So pleased he gave her a kiss on the cheek.

At least one female would be glad to see him return Sunday night.

Well, Mary would be glad—eventually.

Gus hadn't wanted to be his brother's best man.

Ever since he'd bailed out of his own wedding, he'd pretty much headed in the other direction anytime anyone had mentioned words like *best man, wedding, groom, vows, till death do you part.*

So Rance Phillips had stood up for J.D. But Gus had been an usher, and he'd stood close enough to feel like he was right next to J.D. And hearing his brother say the words, Gus felt an odd, inexplicable yearning he hadn't felt before. It seemed to be rooted somewhere deep inside him, and though he felt it there, still knotted up, it didn't feel as tight as it had once been.

He wondered what it would be like to make those vows. And the thought didn't even send him bolting from the church.

Maybe it was seeing the way J.D. looked. He was so... so...so damned *happy!*

Gus wasn't used to his brother being that cheerful.

J.D. had always enjoyed a good time as well as the next guy. But he'd had a chip on his shoulder, too, as long as Gus could remember—one that over the years a lot of guys had tried their best to knock off.

It seemed to Gus that the one who'd finally knocked it off was Lydia—and she'd done it by loving him, not by punching his lights out.

It gave a guy pause for thought.

Gus thought about it a lot. He thought about it during the wedding. He thought about it during the reception. He thought about it when he was lying there alone in what had once been his bedroom in the old Holt ranch house late that night.

And he thought, if it could happen to J.D., maybe it could happen to him. Maybe life wasn't destined to be the way he'd thought it would be at age nineteen. Maybe a guy could grow up and become something more, something better.

He wondered if he could get Mary thinking that way, too. She'd loved him once, and he'd foolishly thrown her love away. Or maybe he hadn't been entirely foolish. Maybe he'd realized he wouldn't know what to do with it if he had it.

He thought he'd know now.

Convincing her was going to be a little trickier.

Gus was good at flirting. Teasing and charming were right up his alley. But he didn't think they'd cut much ice with Mary—not this time.

He'd thought about asking J.D. how he'd managed it with Lydia, but there was never time before the wedding. And after, well, he could hardly tag along on his brother's honeymoon. J.D. was a pretty good brother, but Gus figured even he would draw the line at that!

So he drove back to Taggart's, still weighing his options.

Maybe Taggart could help. After all, he'd presumably courted Felicity. He ought to know how such a thing was done.

But when they were out in the barn after Gus got back late Sunday night, and he asked Taggart, his friend scratched his head and said, "Courted Felicity? Not really. I got set up." He grinned ruefully.

"What do you mean, set up?"

"By Becky."

"Becky?"

Taggart nodded. "Yep. She reckoned I needed a wife. And so she and Susannah figured they'd find me one. And when the two of them put their minds to somethin', boy, a fella's gotta watch out." He winced at the memory.

"Like how?"

"They kept throwin' us together. Becky didn't do her homework so I'd get called in to see her teacher. And they tailed her around, so they'd know where she went and when. Then Becky started in needin' to go here or there. Hell, I couldn't buy a loaf of bread or get my trailer welded or take back a library book without runnin' into Felicity. She thought I was stalkin' her!"

"*Becky* thought of that?"

Taggart nodded. "I used to tell people when she was

little that she made life interesting. Boy, I didn't know the half of it!''

Gus considered that. He didn't think Mary would go for stalking, and since he didn't have an eighth-grader of his own, he couldn't be a concerned parent.

"You got someone in mind?" Taggart asked.

Gus lifted his shoulders. "Maybe."

"Well, ask Beck'. She's a pro," Taggart said cheerfully. "Better you than me," he added, and went off whistling.

Ask Becky to help him do his courting?

Gus would have to think about that.

In the end there were no other options.

And, hey, Becky being a girl, maybe she'd know what sort of thing would appeal. Gus sure didn't. So he volunteered to run errands in town Monday afternoon, and he just happened to time it so he was waiting outside the school when Becky came out to catch the bus.

She did a funny little double take when she saw his truck. He waved her over and, after a split second's hesitation, she hurried in his direction and settled into the truck beside him.

He cleared his throat. "I had somethin' I wanted to talk to you about," he said at last. He cracked his knuckles again.

Becky's head snapped around to look at him. "Talk to me about? Like..." She cleared her throat. "L-like what?"

"Taggart," he began, then stopped. Then started again. "Your dad, I mean...was tellin' me how he and your mom...I mean, Felicity got together. About how you, um, sort of...got them together."

Becky groaned. "I was a kid!" Her face turned bright red.

"He says you did a good job," Gus persisted.

Becky shrugged her back against the seat. "That's nice of him. But I don't see—" She stopped and slanted him a glance. "So what's the, um, favor?"

"How'd you like to...maybe try your hand again?"

Becky's eyes went wide. "What?" Her fingers clenched. "Try my hand at what?"

"At matchmakin'," Gus clarified, feeling like the world's biggest idiot. "For me an' your Miz McLean."

Six

"**Y**ou an'—" Becky seemed to have trouble getting her breath "*—Miz McLean?*" Her astonishment caused Gus to look at her. The color was in fact really high in her cheeks. "But I thought she didn't even like you."

"I told you, we used to know each other."

"I know, but—"

"I used to be engaged to her."

"You an' Miz McLean?"

Gus nodded. He flexed his shoulders, rubbing them against the back of the seat. He turned his gaze back to the road. "A long time ago. I was nineteen. An' we were going to get married an' I...an' I...backed out."

"You dumped Miz McLean?" Becky gaped.

"I didn't *dump* her!" He glared at her, then when she shrank back at his harsh tone, he said, "Sorry," in a quieter voice. "I didn't think I was dumping her," he qualified. "I thought I was savin' us both."

"How'd you figure that?" Becky sounded somewhere between dazed and scornful.

"We were too young. *I* was too young," he modified. "I wasn't ready to settle down. Only I didn't realize it until we were engaged an' things started getting out of hand." His mouth twisted.

Becky looked at him quizzically, as if she wasn't quite sure what that meant.

Gus tugged at his shirt collar, then sighed. "I sorta felt like I was choking. Like the walls were closin' in, you know what I mean?"

Becky scratched her nose. "I think...yeah. Maybe. I guess. Like you think you want somethin', and then when it turns out you might get it, you sorta panic?"

"Exactly," Gus said, and shot her a relieved smile. "How'd you get so smart?"

Becky smiled faintly. "Oh, I guess it happens to everyone."

"Well, it happened to me then," Gus went on. "And I didn't see her for years. Not until that day I came to pick you up. And it was—" he stopped and seemed to grope for the words "—it was, I don't know, just like it used to be, I guess."

Becky's forehead wrinkled. "Huh?"

Gus negotiated his way through the snow drifted along the shoulder of the road to turn onto the rural lane that led to the ranch house. Then he rubbed a hand over his face. "I was hot for her," he muttered.

"Oh." Becky's face turned scarlet.

"Sorry. I shouldn't be layin' all this on you. I'm just tryin' to explain. When I saw Mary again it was like bein' hit between the eyes. It was like nothing had changed. Except me," he added. His mouth twisted. "I grew up. I tried to tell her that, as best I could. Which wasn't very good," he admitted. "But it's true. And, damn it—" he slapped his hand on the steering wheel "—she feels the same way."

"She does?" Becky sounded doubtful.

But Gus was sure. "Yes," he said flatly. "She does. She loves me. I know she does. An' I love her."

Becky didn't say anything. They bounced along up the rutted lane, the wind buffeting the truck. Finally she slanted a glance his way. "So," she said, "if Miz McLean loves you and you love her, what's the problem?"

"The problem is she won't admit it. She's afraid to care again. Afraid I'll hurt her again."

"Will you?"

"No!"

"Just askin'!"

"I'm not hangin' around to hurt her. I love her. I just…need to convince her." His fingers flexed on the steering wheel. "And I'm not doin' a very good job. So, I thought maybe, since you helped your dad and Felicity, maybe you could help me."

"Get you two together?"

"Yes."

"Do you want to marry her?"

That was laying it on the line.

"I—" Gus took a quick harsh breath. "Yes. I do."

It felt like a vow. He meant it like one.

Becky stared out the window. He wondered what she was thinking. He wondered if she thought he was a complete idiot. He couldn't help it.

"Can I ask Susannah to help?" she asked finally.

Susannah? He grimaced. More young women who would know how incompetent he was. Aw, hell, what did it matter as long as he convinced Mary?

"Sure," he said, resigned. "Why not?"

* * *

They decided he had to be subtle.

"Subtle?" Gus said doubtfully.

If he were any more subtle she wouldn't know he was still alive. He hadn't seen Mary since the night he'd brought her home from Bozeman in the snowstorm. He'd debated driving over and banging on her door last night after he'd talked to Becky, but she'd held him off.

"No," she'd said firmly. "You asked me to do this. I'm doing it. I'm talking to Susannah tonight. We'll get back to you."

They'd get back to him!

He had to be insane to put his love life in the hands of a pair of teenage girls!

But then he remembered that, as a teenager, Mary had known a whole heck of a lot more about love than he had. Maybe it came with being a girl. Certainly Becky and Susannah had one happy couple who could provide letters of recommendation.

Still, he was a little dubious when they tracked him down, out by the corral Tuesday afternoon, and laid out their plan.

"She's coming for Thanksgiving dinner," Becky told him.

"And so are you," Susannah continued.

"So you just get me sitting next to her and—"

"No!" Becky said.

"You can't sit next to her," Susannah agreed. "It wouldn't be subtle."

"What's with this subtle?" Gus complained.

"It's what you have to do when you've blown it the first time around," Susannah said bluntly. "Trust us. You have to be casual. Disinterested."

"You can say hello," Becky told him. "But that's all."

"All? You mean I can't—"

Both girls shook their heads. "No!"

"But—"

"Trust us," Becky said again. "There will be a time…"

Gus's eyes narrowed. He looked at them both a little warily. No. *Very* warily. They looked back—two pairs of earnest, shining solemn eyes.

"Trust us."

He sighed—and nodded.

They beamed.

When she'd agreed to go to the Joneses' for Thanksgiving, Mary hadn't given a thought to Gus being there.

Now she couldn't think of anything else.

Of course he would be. She knew, from seeing his truck on Monday afternoon outside the school, that he had not, as she'd hoped, taken off for parts unknown. He had come back.

She'd half expected he would turn up on her doorstep that night.

She went to bed a little later than usual, not wanting to be caught in her nightgown when he did. When he didn't, she'd told herself she was relieved.

Of course she was.

But then she was sure he'd drop by on Tuesday. Or Wednesday.

But he didn't come either day.

And on Wednesday night, she realized why. He would be there on Thanksgiving. He would undoubtedly contrive to sit next to her. And he would make her uncomfortably aware of him the whole time.

She considered calling Felicity and begging off.

She didn't because Gus would know exactly why she

had done it—and she wouldn't give him the satisfaction of being right.

It started to snow while she was making the two pumpkin pies she'd promised to bring. Once more she considered calling and begging off. They all knew she didn't drive well in snow. She didn't want to get stuck out on a rural road somewhere.

The phone rang as she was putting the pies in the oven.

"Hi," Felicity said. "You're not to worry about driving. Someone will come and pick you up."

Gus. Mary was sure.

"It's really not necessary," she began. "I don't want to put anyone out. Don't worry about coming to get me. I have leftovers here."

"Don't be ridiculous. Just be ready at three, okay?"

Mary wanted to say no. She sighed and said, "Okay."

It would be Gus. She was sure it would be Gus. She paced the floor, wrung her hands, went to the bathroom, then did it all over again. She set the pies to cool on the back porch and went back to watch out the front windows for his battered red truck.

And all the while she gave herself a pep talk on how to resist him.

At five minutes to three a gray Ford Explorer turned the corner and plowed up Apple Street to pull to a stop in front of her house. An older man got out and came to the door.

"Mr. Jones?" She gaped, recognizing Taggart's father.

He beamed at her. "Felicity called and asked if me and Ma would stop and pick you up on the way to the ranch."

"Oh! Of course. I'll be ready in a moment." Mary hurried to get the pies and to put on her boots and coat, feeling foolish. She'd been so sure it would be Gus!

Maybe he wasn't going to be there after all.

She didn't have time to wonder. As they drove to the

ranch, Taggart's mother, Gaye, turned around in front and plied her with questions about her pregnancy, wanting to know how she was feeling, when she was due, and assuring her she thought it was a lovely thing she was doing for her sister.

In fact, Gus was there when they got to the ranch. He was waiting, but instead of coming to her, he helped Gaye through the snow to the front door while the girls took the pies. Will carried in the food they had brought, and it was left to Taggart to give Mary his arm.

Thanksgiving at the Joneses' was, Mary soon discovered, a noisy affair.

Besides Taggart and Felicity and their children, Taggart's parents, his partner, Noah Tanner, and all his family, there were twenty-four bull- and bronc-riding students, who were spending the Thanksgiving weekend there at Noah and Taggart's four-day intensive school, there were three other families from the valley—the McCalls, two sets of Nicholses, an older man named Jamison and a birdlike older lady called Maddie Fletcher. There were babies and toddlers, big kids and little ones. There were two more pregnant women—one of the Nichols women, who had lots of dark-red hair, was even bigger than she was. And Brenna McCall, the artist Mary had heard so much about, looked to be about midway there.

Mary wasn't sure what sort of reception the other pregnant women would give her. Some people found her carrying her sister's baby strange and off-putting. But both of them greeted her with warmth and camaraderie.

"You've got to be a saint," the redhead huffed, out of breath from the exertion of just getting across the room, "to do this for someone else. I'm Poppy, by the way. And you're Mary?"

"Come and sit down," Tess Tanner dragged both of

them toward a sofa. "We don't want any babies born here this evening."

"When are you due?" they asked each other simultaneously, then laughed.

"Snap." Poppy grinned. "I'm due in three weeks—if I make it that far."

"I'm not due until February," Mary admitted. "This is just a big baby."

"And there's less of you than there is of me," Poppy said ruefully.

"You look mighty good to me," her husband, Shane, said, bringing them each a glass of milk. He settled down next to Poppy on the sofa and slid his arm around her, pulling her back against him, then proceeded to knead her shoulders.

"Ah!" Poppy smiled and arched her back. "There. And just a little lower. Yes, like that. Mmmmm."

Mary caught herself almost whimpering with envy—and instinctively looked around for Gus.

As if she would ever let him do the same for her!

No way. She berated herself for even thinking it. But still her eyes sought him—and found him on the far side of the room, hoisting a beer with a group of the students from the school—including both of the very svelte and curvy cowgirls. He hadn't done more than glance in her direction since she'd arrived.

So much for wanting her.

He barely seemed to know she was there.

Gus knew where she was every single moment.

And it was all he could do not to push his way through the throng of people and take his place beside her.

"Are you sure about this?" he said through his teeth to

Becky when she passed, carrying a bowl of cranberry sauce to the table. He didn't like *subtle* very much at all.

But Becky didn't bat an eye or so much as glance in Mary's direction. "Of course we're sure."

Gus wasn't. He hadn't liked leaving her to Taggart to shepherd in from the car. He didn't like letting Shane get her a glass of milk. He didn't have the slightest interest in either one of those annoying wannabe cowgirls from the bronc-riding class who kept cozying up to him and trying their female wiles out on him.

He ground his teeth.

Tess came by and put him to work stirring the gravy in the kitchen. Then he had to fill water glasses and mop up Clay Tanner's spilled milk.

By the time Gus got through the buffet line he wasn't only not sitting at Mary's table. He wasn't even sitting in the same room.

He glared at Becky when her eyes met his across the room, but she just smiled, then turned back to talk to Tuck McCall.

Watching them, Gus was reminded of when he and Mary had first become a couple.

They hadn't been all that much older than Becky and Tuck.

It didn't seem possible, Becky and Tuck looked so incredibly *young!* How could he have thought he was serious about a girl at that age?

And yet he had been.

He'd dreamed about Mary every night. He'd thought about her every day. Part of it, granted, had been hormones. But there had been a lot of girls willing to assuage what their health ed teacher, Mrs. Plum, had called his "masculine needs."

But Gus hadn't taken them up on it.

It had damned near killed him, but he'd waited for Mary—until she was ready, until she was convinced they were going to be a couple—forever.

He'd thought they were.

He hadn't realized how fickle he could be—how tempting the horizon would become, how vast the still-unexplored world would seem.

Mrs. Plum had warned them.

"Biology is not all!" she'd said like she was handing down a universal truth. "Emotions matter, too.

"The hard part is getting them coordinated," she'd gone on. She'd lectured them at length, talking not just about sex and reproduction, but about relationships. She'd probably said a whole lot more than most school boards would have approved.

Not that her students had listened.

Or not that Gus had, anyway.

He'd been a kid—and he'd acted like one.

"Food's not that bad, is it?" Felicity settled down beside him and looked at his untouched plate.

"Not bad at all," Gus assured her. "It's fantastic."

"You can tell by looking? You haven't touched it."

He reddened. "I'll eat. I was just…thinking."

She patted his knee and smiled knowingly. "Good for you, Gus."

He dug into the food on his plate, slanting her a glance, trying to decide if Becky had told Felicity she was match-making for him.

But she didn't say anything further. Instead she started asking him about some of the students he'd been working with in bronc riding. Did he think any of them had potential? Did he enjoy teaching? Was he going to go back into competition next year?

Out of the corner of his eye he saw Mary pass through

the room, three eager young cowboys creating a wedge like a football special team so she could move through the crowded room unscathed. Gus's eyes followed her, and he didn't answer Felicity's question until she repeated it patiently. Then he stammered something that he hoped made sense.

He didn't know if he was going back to compete next year, so he could hardly say.

Hell, he didn't know what he was going to do next week.

Felicity cleaned her plate, then stood up. "Once everyone is finished, I think we'll have to mix things up a little, make sure all you cowpokes don't just stand around talking about horses and bulls. How are you at parlor games?"

Gus looked up, horrified. "What?"

Mary had never laughed so much in her life.

By the time they'd split into teams and worked their way through song-title charades and she'd watched one cowboy pantomime "Hark, The Herald Angels Sing" and another do his best with "Itsy-Bitsy Teeny-Weeny Yellow Polka Dot Bikini," she thought she might wet her pants or have the baby right there on the sofa.

Then Tess suggested a different game—word associations, this time—and she divided them into teams.

"You draw a card," she instructed Mace, "and you have to get the people on your team to guess what the word is on your card, but you can't say any of the words listed below it. And you have a minute to do it. Go."

He looked at it a moment, then at his wife who was sitting next to Mary on the sofa.

"Come on," his brother urged as the timer ticked on. 'Say somethin'! Time's a-wasting."

Mace ignored him, his eyes still on Jenny. "What you always wanted to be—besides my wife," he said softly.

The smile that touched Jenny's face was radiant. "Mother."

A grin split Mace's face. "One point for our side."

Some of the words drawn were easy. Some were hard.

Mary guessed right when she said, "Rope," to Noah's "What headers and heelers use." Gus and half a dozen other cowboys were guessing *lariat* and *lasso*.

"They do so use a lasso," Gus said indignantly when Noah said, "No!" to him.

"That wasn't the word Noah was looking for," Tess explained. "Last card." She handed it to Mary.

Oh, heavens.

For a moment, as Mary stared at it, her mind went blank. She couldn't say *fruit*. She couldn't say *prune in a previous life*. She couldn't say *purple*. She couldn't say *sugar* or *fairy*.

"Come on!" Shane urged.

"Hurry up," said Mace.

She looked up desperately and saw everyone staring at her, waiting.

Her eyes found Gus. "Health ed teacher," she said. "Biology is not all!"

In the stunned silence that followed, she turned bright-red.

"Huh?" said Noah and Mace and Felicity and Taggart and half a dozen others.

"What?" said Shane and Poppy and Jenny and the rest.

All but one.

"Plum!" Gus said, triumphant.

Their eyes met.

And Mary nodded. "Yes."

The Thanksgiving party swirled on. More games followed, then music, to which Shane whirled his very pregnant wife into a two-step that continued until they were laughing so hard they had to sit down or, "I'm going to have this baby right here!" Poppy threatened, which sobered her husband at once.

"You're not!"

Poppy, smiling, said meekly, "I'll try not."

But her words took the wind out of Shane's sails. He settled her on the sofa and put her feet up in his lap.

Gus, watching, would have liked to do the same thing to Mary. He'd connected with her—at last. Over Mrs. Plum, of all the crazy things!

Everyone else had been dumbstruck.

"How on earth do you get *plum* out of that?" Noah had asked.

"They have a past, Daddy," Susannah had explained. "Like you and Mom."

"Not exactly," Gus had said hastily, worried about how Mary would take that. But she didn't seem upset. She was still smiling. At him.

She kept right on smiling the rest of the evening, and she stayed a lot longer than he figured she would. But as the crowd thinned out and more and more people left, she got up, too.

"I really ought to go," she said apologetically to Felicity and Taggart. "I realize that your parents are staying. But even though I came with them, I need to get home."

"Oh, of course!" Felicity said.

"I'll take you," Taggart said promptly.

"No!" Becky blurted. Then, face red, she said, "I mean…I need you to help me with my math."

Taggart gaped. "Help you? With your math? Tonight?"

Becky bobbed her head earnestly. "I've got a lot, an' I don't understand it, an'—"

Susannah's foot collided with Gus's ankle. "Now!"

Gus almost missed his cue. "I'll take you," he managed,

and at Mary's startled blink he shrugged. "I'm lousy at math."

Felicity beamed. "That would be great." Then she turned to her stepdaughter and gave her an arch smile. "We certainly wouldn't want Becky to do poorly in math."

Becky's face got even redder. "I'm just tryin' to stay on top of things, like you said. I'll get my book," she said to her father.

She started toward the stairs, then stopped and shot a quick look at Gus and Mary. "G'night, Miz McLean."

She touched his arm as she slipped past and mouthed, "Good luck."

Seven

They went outside into the cold and the snow and the silence.

Gus had hold of her arm so she couldn't slip and take a fall. His grasp was firm but gentle. He held her carefully—the same way she'd seen Shane hold on to Poppy when they'd left a while ago.

"You okay?" His breath was warm against her ear.

"Yes. Fine." She could feel the heat of his body through both of their jackets as they picked their way through the snow toward his truck. He hovered. Solicitous. Gentle. Caring.

Gus.

Mary tried to distance herself from this version of Gus Holt. It was far too close to the one she'd dreamed of all those years ago.

But it was hard to pretend it wasn't happening when it very definitely was.

His fingers tightened on her arm. "Be careful," he cautioned. "The ground's uneven."

She tried to be careful—and not just of her footing. Of her heart.

Gus opened the door to his truck and helped her in. He reached around her and fastened her seat belt because he had a better angle at it than she did. His hat brim brushed her chin as he did so.

"Sorry."

Mary ran her tongue over her lips. "It's all right."

He went around and got in, starting the truck, then turning up the heater full blast. "There's a blanket in the back if you want it."

She shook her head. "I'm fine." She gave him a bright smile.

The look he gave her in return was grave.

"Is something wrong?" she asked. "If you'd rather not take me—"

"Of course I'm taking you," he cut her off. He flicked on the windshield wipers and put the truck in reverse, then concentrated on getting the truck turned around and headed down the lane toward the county road.

But he didn't speak. Didn't say a word. Mary wondered at that, then decided it was better that way. If he left the conversation up to her, she could direct it however she wanted—which would be into safe, impersonal lanes.

She settled back against the seat, took a deep breath, then let it out slowly. She watched Gus out of the corner of her eye. He had his own gaze firmly on the snow-covered lane.

"It was a lovely Thanksgiving," she ventured finally.

"Yeah."

They wound down the narrow, winding road. The world seemed all shades of silver and gray and black. Only the snow sparkled white in the glare of the headlights. She rubbed her belly. "I'm stuffed," she said. "Aren't you? Such wonderful food. And so much of it."

"There was a lot."

"I should never have had that piece of pie. I don't know why I did. I certainly didn't need it." She prattled on about the dinner, the people, the games all the way to town. Gus managed the occasional monosyllable, only in response to direct questions on her part.

More than once she slanted him a glance, wondering at his taciturnity. It wasn't like Gus to have nothing to say.

They pulled up in front of her house, and she fumbled to undo the seat belt. He reached over and did it for her, then jumped out and came around to give her his arm up the walk.

"I can manage," she protested, but in fact was glad of the support.

She put the key in the lock and turned it, then pushed open the door and turned to say good-night to him. "Thank you," she said.

"Could I have a cup of coffee?"

She blinked.

"I need a cup of coffee," he said. "And we need to talk."

"No, I—"

"About Mrs. Plum."

"Mrs. Plum?"

He nodded. "Coffee," he said. "Then talk." He turned her around and steered her into the house, then shut the door and helped her off with her jacket.

She tried to toe her boots off.

"Hold still," he commanded, and dropped to one knee to lift her feet one at a time and slip her boots off for her while she held on to the pillar beside the entry to the living room with one hand and braced the other on Gus's shoulder. It was strong, firm, steady.

She was trembling.

He looked up. "Cold?"

"No. Yes. I don't know."

He finished with her boots, then snagged the moccasins she wore in the house and tucked her feet into them. His fingers on her feet made her tremble even more. When he stood up she stepped back quickly. But he just pointed her toward the sofa. "Sit down and wrap up in that afghan. I'll make the coffee."

"I can."

"I'll do it."

"But—"

"Go. Sit."

"When did you get so bossy?" she grumbled even as she padded across the room and settled on the sofa, tucking her feet under her.

Gus just smiled enigmatically and disappeared into the kitchen.

Teasing and flirting, Gus knew, were fine, as far as they got you. Subtle was fine, too. It had got him here.

But in the end, it all came down to this.

Spilling his guts. Telling it like it was.

Laying his heart on the line.

Gus took his time making the coffee, trying to rehearse the words. They were there, as inarticulate as they were imperative, on the tip of his tongue.

He muttered them, fumbled with them, trying to express them in his mind, but finally he gave up.

Muscle memory was one thing. Soul baring was something else. He'd never been good at this kind of preparation. And unlike Becky, he couldn't rehearse.

Suddenly he didn't want to wait any longer.

Suddenly he knew there was no time like the present. Suddenly he had to tell her what, finally—this evening— he'd really understood.

He drummed his fingers on the counter now, impatient for the coffee to drip. It was decaf. He didn't care. He didn't need caffeine now. He had nerves enough.

He could have gone back to face her without it. But, for all that he was going to have to do this extemporaneously, he still wanted a mug to hang on to.

At last it was ready. He poured two mugs full, added milk to hers, then carried them back to the living room.

Mary was curled on the couch and she looked as if she were asleep. But when he came in, her eyes flicked open at once and she straightened to sit up.

"Don't," he said. "Relax. Here." He handed her one mug and then, tossing his hat onto the chair, sat down at the other end of the couch.

Mary tucked her feet more closely beneath her, careful to leave more than a foot of space between them. She brought the cup to her lips and took a sip. Her eyes watched him from above the rim of the cup. She didn't say anything.

Gus didn't quite know where to begin.

In the old days he'd never had any problem talking to Mary, but things were different now. Maybe, he reflected, because he wasn't just talking—he was thinking before he spoke.

"I was thinking about Mrs. Plum," he began.

Mary smiled. "That was wonderful! I'm glad you remembered. I didn't know if you would. But I didn't know any other words—"

"Before you brought her up," he cut in firmly. "I was thinking about her earlier—when I was watching Becky and Tuck across the room."

Mary looked surprised at his interruption, but she pressed the mug against her lips and didn't say anything else.

Gus, feeling her gaze on him, swallowed. "I was thinking about how young they are—Becky and Tuck. And then I was thinking about how young *we* were when we first started going out." He flexed his fingers on the handle of the mug. That was why he'd wanted it—to have something to hang on to. He stretched his booted feet out in front of him and studied the toes.

Mary waited, not saying a word.

"I thought about the way things were between us—you wantin' a home and a family and the whole works…and me wantin'…sex." He sat up straight and looked at her urgently. "It wasn't just sex, Mar'. I loved you. As much as I knew how. But I didn't know much about love in those days, though I guess I thought I did. But I know better now. And I started thinking about ol' Plum. About what she said." He settled back again and flexed his toes inside his boots. He balanced the mug on his belt buckle and stared at it.

"What she said?" Mary prompted after a moment. "You mean about biology not being all?"

"Yeah." He nodded. "It's true, I can see that now from hindsight. Biology isn't the only thing, but when you're sixteen or seventeen it feels like everything. Did to me, anyway. I was a walking hard-on in those days," he muttered, embarrassed as he remembered how all-consuming his biological urges had been.

"You were…eager," Mary agreed with a faint smile.

"I was," Gus agreed grimly. "And I really didn't stop to think that it was different for you. I didn't know it was—until we were engaged."

"What do you mean?"

"I mean, when we got engaged, I thought we were on

the same page, that we wanted the same things. Each other, you know? Makin' love—spending nights together and not havin' to sneak around. That's what I thought I was getting when I asked you to marry me. That's what I thought *love* was.'' He shook his head. ''I wasn't thinking about it bein'…I don't know…a relationship—'' He twisted the word when he spoke ''I didn't think about commitment. Or about bein' together…forever. It didn't even occur to me.''

''It didn't?'' She stared at him, eyes wide.

''Nope. Didn't even cross my mind.''

Her jaw sagged slightly.

''Guys don't think like that, Mar'. Not most of 'em anyway. Not when they're eighteen, nineteen years old. They're pretty much thinkin' with their—'' he felt his face heat ''—well, you know what they're thinkin' with. You remember what *I* was thinkin' with! Then, when the wedding got closer and you started talkin' about apartments and leases and if we should try to save money to buy some land or if I was gonna maybe go into trainin' horses with J.D. and my dad—''

Even now, thinking about how he'd felt then had the power to dry his mouth and make his breath come in short, shallow gulps. ''Buyin' land and settlin' down and raisin' horses wasn't what I was thinkin' about at all. It sounded—'' he took another breath ''—I don't know… responsible. And it scared the bejeezus outa me.

''I thought, 'I don't wanta be on a ranch the rest of my life. I don't even know what it's like in California, Arizona, Louisiana.' I'd never been to half the places I wanted to go! Hadn't done half the things I wanted to do! And the closer the time came and the more you talked about the wedding and…and after…I couldn't see myself ever gettin' to do 'em. Not if…not if we got married. It was what you wanted, what you were lookin' for, hopin' for...and it wasn't what I wanted at all.''

It was the conversation they'd never had twelve years ago, the explanation, lame as it was, that he'd never managed to give.

It wasn't admirable even now, to Gus's way of thinking.

But it was a little better thought out, a little clearer than his desperate, ''I can't marry you. I might as well be dead,'' or whatever awful words he'd come up with on that pay phone.

''I'm sorry,'' he said now. ''Sorry I was such a jerk.''

Their gazes met for just a moment. Then Mary's dropped. She stared into the coffee steaming in her mug. She stared and stared. Gus saw her swallow.

And then she began to speak, her words so soft Gus had to strain to hear. ''I wanted to die,'' she told him. ''Of pain. Of mortification. Of embarrassment. Of being so *wrong* about you! I didn't understand at all. I felt betrayed.''

''You were betrayed.''

But she shook her head. ''No. You were a boy. Not a man.''

He winced at that, true though it was.

She didn't notice. She went right on. ''And I—I didn't understand. I thought...I thought just what you said—that we were a couple, that we loved each other—''

''We did!''

''—and that that meant we were going to be together forever. That we were going to have babies together, build a life together, make a home together. I should have realized.'' She shook her head.

''How could you? I didn't realize! We were kids!''

''Still,'' she said stubbornly. ''I should have known.''

She looked at him. "I should have seen it coming that day we went to get the marriage license."

"We didn't get a marriage license."

"I know. But we were going to. We went to the courthouse, remember? We went up to the office and asked for the papers and you wouldn't fill them out."

"Because of my name! They wanted me to put down my name!"

"Exactly. And you wouldn't do it. You wanted to put your initials."

"There's nothin' wrong with initials." He glared at her. "Nothin' at all wrong with D.A."

"But it's not your name."

"I wish my name wasn't my name!"

"What is it?"

He shook his head. He wasn't answering that. He'd never answered that. His knuckles were white on his coffee mug. It was the deepest, darkest secret of his life. "Don't matter," he said gruffly.

Mary smiled sadly. "But it does, you see? Because you don't trust me."

"That's not true!" He set down the coffee mug and bounced up off the couch, pacing around the room. "I do trust you."

"But not enough to tell me your first name."

"I don't go by it! I never have, you know that. Besides, it's not a big deal. It's an old family name, and it doesn't mean anything."

"Except to you."

He glowered at her, rubbed a hand through his hair and wished to hell she hadn't brought that up. His first name didn't matter. He'd never used it. And it wasn't true that he didn't trust her, he just hadn't seen the point of putting it on a legal document.

"But you're right now. It doesn't matter anymore," she said now. "It's over. Past. Done. It's been done for years."

That stopped his pacing. He shook his head. "No. It isn't. It's still here. Between us."

"This *want* you've been talking about?"

"Yes. It's still there. You feel it. I feel it."

"Of course. It's what Mrs. Plum said—biology. We'll always feel it."

He shook his head impatiently. "It's not only that. That's what I'm trying to tell you. It's more."

"What do you mean more?" Her eyes narrowed, pinning him with their intensity.

"I mean I want those other things, too! I want the…the relationship. The commitment." He ran his tongue over his lips. "The…kids. The mortgage. The future. Forever. The whole shebang." He met her stare with an equally intent one of his own.

"The whole…shebang," Mary repeated slowly. She was regarding him with a sort of wary fascination.

At least, Gus thought, she hadn't told him to get lost.

He poked his chest. "It's here now, too. That emotion thing. What you had all along. At least, I guess it's what you had," he added truthfully.

"You guess?"

"Well, I'm not a girl, am I? I don't know how girls think. But ol' Plum talked about emotional needs, about them bein' as important as the biological ones. And…well, that's where I am now. Finally. I never really understood that before. But…well, I do now. I have 'em, too."

For a long moment Mary just stared at him. Finally she blinked. But she still didn't say a word.

Gus shifted under her gaze. He didn't like her looking at him that way—like he'd grown another head or something. "It's true!" he protested. "That's why I'm here."

"Because now you feel the way I feel...felt," Mary corrected herself. "You think," she added dubiously.

"Yeah, I do." Gus lifted his chin stubbornly.

"And that means what? That you want to get married?" He gulped. Then, "Yeah," he said. "I would."

"To me." It wasn't precisely a question, and yet it was.

"Of course, to you!"

"Why?"

"Because I love you."

"Gus, you just got through telling me you don't know what love means."

"I said I *didn't* know what it meant. When I was nineteen, I didn't know what it meant. I do now."

"What?"

He frowned at her. "What do you mean, what?"

"What does it mean?" she asked patiently.

"It means..." he stopped. He ran his tongue over his lips, trying to find the words to say what in his gut he understood. "It means," he said finally, "puttin' the other person first. Caring about what they need more than what I need. Wanting to do what's best for them."

He met her a wide blue eyes steadily and doggedly. If this was a test, he was giving her the whole answer, the whole nine yards—and then some. "It means wanting that, not just now but forever. When it isn't easy. When it isn't fun. When it sometimes doesn't even feel good. Because bein' with that person—bein' with *you* is worth more than all the other stuff I used to think I'd rather be doin'." He shook his head. "I wanted that other stuff then. I wasn't ready then. I am now. I swear."

She didn't speak. She stared at him as if she were dumbstruck.

Then she blinked rapidly and gave a little shake of her head. Her fingers clenched on the mug in her hands, and her gaze dropped and she stared down into it. "Hell," she muttered softly. "Oh, hell."

He took three long strides across the room and hunkered down in front of her so that, if she would just lift her gaze, they would be on eye level. He put his hands on her knees. "What's that mean? 'Oh, hell'?"

She gave a small shudder and looked up at him, still blinking. "It means exactly what I said. Oh, hell. I didn't want you to have a good answer. I didn't want you to say the right words." She turned her head away and wouldn't look at him.

He took the mug from her and set it aside. Then he grasped her hands in his, silently urging her to look at him. "Mary?"

Still she wouldn't. She gave a quick hard shake of her head. "No, Gus. Go away."

"I love you, Mar'."

She shut her eyes.

"I want to marry you, Mar'. I want to be there for you. I want us to have all that stuff you wanted all those years ago."

She tugged her hands out of his and crossed her arms over her breasts, tucking her hands away so he couldn't hold them. "No," she said, her tone agonized. "You can't."

"But I do. Don't you?"

She opened her eyes and looked at him squarely then. "I can't, Gus. I can't go through it again."

"Why not?" Hadn't he just said everything she wanted him to?

"Because," she said flatly, "I don't trust you."

He stared at her, shocked.

Then he realized he had no right to be. Why, after all, should she trust him? She'd trusted him once, and he'd walked out on her. No. Worse. He hadn't even walked out. He'd asked her to marry him, and then, when he'd panicked, he hadn't even had the decency to come back and tell her face-to-face. He'd blurted something over a long-distance phone line, then took off back to his buddies and the next rodeo. He'd left her to make excuses, to cancel everything, to face the people he'd never bothered to face.

He bent his head, shut his eyes, and hoped the Almighty listened to cowboys who took a dozen years to wake up and smell the coffee. Then he got to his feet and stood looking down at her, waiting until she looked up at him.

When she did, he smiled a little wryly. "Fair enough. I guess I'll just have to teach you to trust me, Mar'."

Mary heard the front door close with a soft click.

Then she heard nothing save the sound of the old mantel clock's ponderous tick, tick. And then she heard a truck door shut. An engine started.

And at last she heard him drive away.

She took a huge, desperate gulp of air. And it wasn't until she'd let it out again with a shudder that shook her to her toes that she realized she must have been holding her breath.

The baby within nudged her belly. A small poke of reality.

Thank God, she thought, patting it absently and taking another shaky breath and exhaling again.

"Gus," she murmured. His name seemed to tremble on her lips. "Oh, Gus. How could you? How could you do this to me?"

She wanted to blot it all out. To pretend he hadn't come, that he hadn't said the things he had, that she hadn't heard from his lips all the things she'd once longed to hear him say.

Please, dear God, she didn't want to fall in love with him again.

He might say all the right things, but talk was cheap. Gus was Gus—and, to quote the old cliché, a leopard didn't change his spots. How could she trust him?

How?

She couldn't. Couldn't afford to.

But what her mind told her and what her heart heard were two different things. Her mind could steel itself against him. Her heart was another story.

When she went to bed that night she was afraid.

He called her the next morning.

"I've only got a minute. We're buckin' horses again soon as we finish a quick break. But I wanted to see how you were." His voice was soft, concerned.

And Mary, who had been padding around the house telling herself that in the bright light of day she would know better than to succumb to his charm, said briskly, "I'm fine."

"Good. Got plans for tonight?"

"I'm having leftovers at my neighbor Cloris's. She's a retired teacher, and she gets lonely. Her family came for the holiday but they're gone now so she invited me over."

"Think she'd invite me, too? What's her number?"

"You can't just call up someone you don't know and invite yourself for a meal!"

"I'm not invitin' myself. I'm askin' her to invite me."

"Well, I won't give you her number."

"Okay, make it difficult," Gus said cheerfully. "See you tonight."

"Gus!"

But he had already hung up.

Mary put down the phone and shook her head. See, she

told herself, he hadn't changed. He was still Gus, through and through. Going after what he wanted come hell or high water. Well, he wouldn't run over Cloris Steadman, of that she was sure.

As it turned out, he didn't have to. Cloris apparently simply opened the door and ushered him in!

He was sitting in her living room, entertaining her and Alice Benn with rodeo stories, when Mary arrived. He got up at once and helped her off with her jacket.

"I'd have stopped to get you," he said, "but I thought you might already be here."

"You were afraid I wouldn't let you come with me," Mary said tartly, shaking out her hair and trying not to answer his grin with one of her own.

"That, too," Gus agreed. "You look gorgeous."

The appreciative sighs of Cloris and Alice were audible all the way across the room. Mary shot them a hard look. They beamed at her.

"So nice your young man was able to come, too," Alice said. She patted the sofa next to her. "When Cloris invited you, we didn't realize he was in town."

"He's *not* my young man," Mary objected, going to sit beside Alice. "And he's not in town. He's living out at Taggart's."

"That's what he was telling us. He said that Noah told him there's enough work between the schools here and the ones they do on the road that he can stay on permanently. I'll bet you're pleased!" Alice beamed, and Cloris, on her way to the kitchen, gave Mary a thumbs-up sign.

Mary's eyes widened. She felt an odd flutter in her middle that, for once, she didn't think had anything to do with the baby. She turned to Gus. "What do you mean, permanent?"

A corner of his mouth lifted. "Something about the word

you don't understand? It's pretty straightforward. It means, basically, from here on out."

"Live here, you mean? You're going to *live* at Taggart's?"

"For now." He lifted his shoulders. "I was thinkin' maybe I could get my own place before long." His eyes were smiling at her.

"What about your itchy feet? What about going down the road? What about that horizon you're always heading toward? What about feeling smothered when you stay in one spot?" She dragged up every single example she could remember of his earlier view of how he wanted to live his life.

"Reckon I've seen enough horizons for a while," he said easily. "And I'm gettin' a little old to be goin' down the road all year long. Rodeo's a young man's game."

"You're not old!"

"Not yet. But I'm gettin' there. And I like a pillow and a mattress more'n I ever thought I would. A guy gets a crick in his neck, he sleeps too many nights in his truck. No, I think settlin' down is gonna suit me fine." He looked positively cheerful at the thought.

Mary wished she believed it—or maybe she wished she did not!

She didn't know what she wished. She got to her feet quickly. "I'm going to go see what I can do to help Cloris in the kitchen."

"You can't do anything for Cloris in the kitchen," Cloris said, having overheard. "Dinner is ready. Everyone come and eat. Gus, we're having the half of the turkey that didn't get eaten last night when the family was here. Will you carve?"

He looked momentarily nonplussed, then nodded. "Sure. I'll do my best."

He did his best all evening. And, Mary had to admit, when it came to charming old ladies—or young ladies or any ladies, for that matter—Gus Holt's best was very, very good.

He told them stories about Mary growing up that had her blushing and trying to kick him under the table. She blushed even worse when it turned out to be Alice's ankle she connected with and the older woman gave a startled, "Oh! What was that?"

"Sorry," Mary muttered, mortified.

Gus laughed, delighted, and Cloris and Alice looked at each other across the table and smiled like conspirators.

Mary gave up protesting and focused on her meal. There was no point, she told herself. Gus at his most charming was simply too much of a force to overcome.

Her best hope was that he would burn bright, then fade fast. That's what she'd do—she would simply sit back and wait.

Decision made, she simply made up her mind to enjoy him, to laugh at his stories, to take his compliments with a smile, to accept his solicitous behavior, his fetching and carrying of cups of tea and plates of pie. And when, after dinner, he said he would walk her home, she didn't demur.

She even permitted herself to enjoy his escort. Her balance, since the baby had gotten so much bigger, was not too reliable, and the path between her house and Cloris's wasn't well cleared.

"You go see her a lot?" Gus asked as they went up her steps.

"Fairly often. She gets lonely otherwise. She's alone. Her children are in Billings and Cheyenne." She turned on the top step to thank him and to say goodbye to him there, hoping she would be able to prevent him from following her in.

But Gus just said, "Got a shovel? Give it to me. I'll clear you a path."

She supposed she should have objected, but it would be nice to have the way better shoveled, and she certainly wasn't up to doing it. "Thanks."

Gus went down the steps with the shovel. Mary shut the door. Resolutely she walked into the living room and opened her briefcase. She had a set of papers to grade. No time like the present.

And it would keep her from standing by the window, staring out, watching Gus.

It would give her time to think of a reason not to let him in when he came back. She had no doubt he'd be angling to.

She took the papers out to the kitchen and spread them out on the table and began to work. Outside she could hear the scritch, scritch of the shovel moving the snow. She had to steel herself to stay put, not to go watch Gus.

"Why would you want to watch a man shovel snow?" she asked herself in a disgusted mutter.

Because the man was Gus.

That was the answer. And she didn't like it. But the fact was, watching Gus do anything physical was a treat. He was so capable, so confident, so in control of his body. Whether it was riding a bronc, changing a tire or pitching hay, he drew the eye.

At least he'd always drawn her eye.

She forced her eyes back to the paper she was grading.

The phone rang.

"I wish you had come for Thanksgiving," Ruthie said. "I want to see you. I want to see how big you've gotten."

"Big," Mary said. "I'll have someone take a picture."

"It's not the same. You're coming for Christmas, aren't you?"

"The doctor said it would be better to stick around the last couple of months. And the weather is unpredictable. We don't have those eighty-degree days you do."

"You shouldn't have left." It was becoming Ruthie's mantra.

"I needed a job and I wanted to come back to Montana," Mary said. It was her own mantra.

"And you didn't want me breathing down your neck." Ruthie wasn't stupid.

"I thought it would be better for both of us."

"And you were probably right," Ruthie admitted. "But I still wish you were here. I'm quitting February 1st. I've told Jeff we're coming up a week before your due date so we'll be sure to be there in time. If the doctor thinks it's going to be early, you let me know. We've got reservations, but we can change them. I don't want to miss it. I can't wait. I'm taking classes. Lamaze classes. So I can coach you."

"You'll be better prepared than I am." Outside she could hear the clump of Gus's boots on the porch.

"Haven't you started yet?" Ruthie asked.

"I've got two and a half months left to get ready."

The door opened and Gus came in, his tanned face slightly flushed from the exertion. There was a dusting of snowflakes on his shoulders and his hat, and a lopsided seductive Gus Holt grin on his face. He looked seriously gorgeous and he wasn't even really trying.

Mary swallowed hard. If he could make her knees quiver for no reason at all, she was in very deep trouble indeed.

"I need to go," she said to Ruthie. "I'll call you later."

"But—"

"Later," Mary promised and hung up. She needed all her wits about her to deal with Gus. If she kept on talking to her sister, she was fairly sure that the next time she looked around Gus would be in her bed.

She took a deep breath and laced her fingers together, then pasted a bright I'm-your-friend smile on her own face. "Well," she said briskly. "That was very kind. Thank you so much."

Gus's grin just got wider. "Tryin' to get rid of me, Mar'?"

"Yes." She beamed determinedly. "Is it working?"

He laughed. "For the moment," he said, surprising her.

He took three steps across the kitchen until he was close enough that his jacket brushed the front of her shirt, close enough that she could see the beat of the pulse in his throat, close enough that she could have counted each individual whisker on his jaw. She would have backed up, but the table was behind her.

"Hold still," he said, his voice soft and rough at the same time. He touched her chin with his hand and then, her mouth with his lips. His nose was cold but his mouth was warm as he tasted her gently. Tenderly. Softly.

Mary swallowed a moan.

Then all at once, he stepped back and smiled a little crookedly. "Love you, Mar'."

And as she tried desperately to shore up her trampled defenses, he left.

Eight

It was the hardest thing he'd ever done—walking away like that, not pressing his advantage, not taking her into his arms and kissing her with the urgency he felt.

"Don't forget about subtle," Becky had told him that morning. She and Susannah had come to watch Gus's students ride broncs, and whenever he had a free minute, they continued their counseling.

"Just 'cause you're doin' good, don't think you can bowl her over," Susannah said.

"I'm not tryin' to bowl her over," he'd said. "I just know what I want."

"But Miz McLean doesn't know what she wants yet," Becky had put in.

"She wants me."

"But she doesn't want to," Susannah had explained, as if he were some flunk-out from courtship school. "So you have to let her want to on her own terms."

"How?" How in heaven's name could he let her come to him on her terms if he wasn't there?

That was when they'd agreed it was okay for him to get himself invited to Cloris Steadman's for dinner.

"But that's all," Becky had said. "Nothing else. Then you come home."

"Nothing?"

"You can walk her home," Susannah said. "That's it."

He wasn't going to be reduced to begging to be allowed to kiss Mary. He knew what they'd say. He'd grumbled. And frankly he hadn't thought much of their game plan, but his own was pretty shaky.

So he'd done what they said—more or less. He'd walked Mary home. The shoveling bit had been improvisation. But it had seemed like a smart move.

Doing more than that, he realized, was not. So when his gut and all his instincts told him to press for more, he'd done what Becky and Susannah said.

He'd backed off.

"You've got to leave her wanting you," they'd told him, nodding sagely, as if they had all the answers, these two pip-squeak matchmakers.

So he'd left—and hoped to heck he'd left her wanting him.

He sure as hell was wanting her!

He wanted to go back the next night after he'd finished with the bronc riders.

"No," Becky and Susannah decided. In fact, they barred his way to his truck. "It's too soon."

It wasn't too soon as far as Gus was concerned! He'd been thinking about Mary all day. He'd barely slept a wink all night just thinking about her, remembering how soft her lips had been under his, thinking about how much more they could have done. He'd been anticipating it all day.

He scowled at the girls who stood, arms folded across their chests, between him and his truck. "It's Saturday night! Date night! I could just drop in. Casual-like."

"No."

"She might be expecting me."

"She won't be. Unless you said you'd be there." Becky's green eyes accused him.

"I didn't say I would be there." He tried to look righteous and proper. He did not tell the girls he'd kissed Mary. They wouldn't have understood how a fella could just stand so much temptation. "I can't even call her?"

"No."

"But—"

"No."

He glared at them. This wasn't what he'd had in mind when he'd asked for help. "You're supposed to be figuring out how to get us together, not keep us apart," he complained.

They just looked back at him impassively.

"You like watchin' me suffer," he muttered.

"Maybe a little," Susannah agreed cheerfully.

"No, we don't. Not really," Becky said earnestly. "It'll work out in the end, Gus," she promised. "Really it will."

"How do you know? This isn't what you did for your old man. What makes you such experts?"

"We're women," Susannah said simply.

He couldn't argue with that.

"I don't have to do this a long time, do I?" he asked Becky.

"Not long. Maybe a week."

"A *week?*"

Becky shrugged narrow shoulders. "She knows you care, right? So she's expectin' you to be there. Looking for you. Waiting."

Was she? Gus wasn't sure he dared hope.

"So you gotta wait a little," Becky explained. "Be just a little hard to get—just right now—so she'll miss you. You can help me with my homework."

She missed him.

It was perverse. Ridiculous. Foolish in the extreme.

She shouldn't even be thinking about Gus Holt. But she was. She thought about him a lot—24/7, or so it seemed.

She remembered his kiss—and his words. "Love you, Mar'."

And she found herself expecting to hear his boots on her steps on Saturday evening after he got done with bronc-riding school. But eight o'clock turned into nine o'clock and nine got close to ten and still he didn't come.

He hadn't said he would, of course. And she didn't really care.

But he'd said he loved her!

She paced around the little house. She poked her head between the curtains to stare down the hill toward the high-way. She scanned the street for battered red pickup trucks.

There were no signs of Gus anywhere.

Well, fine. So much for loving her.

He was probably out carousing with his buddies. She wondered if he was over at the Dew Drop this very minute. Not that she cared!

Still, something made her go and put on her heavy jacket and do the contortions necessary to stick her feet into her boots. Then she went out for a walk. It was time to return a magazine she'd borrowed from Alice last weekend. She'd had it longer than she expected.

It had nothing to do with Alice's house being on the street behind the Dew Drop.

Gus had done a marvelous job of shoveling her a path

to Cloris's. And from there Mr. Gilliam had continued. So she didn't have any trouble reaching Alice's place. But when she got there, all the lights were off.

Not surprising, really, as it was after ten. Well, she would leave the magazine inside Alice's storm door, then continue on her constitutional. It wouldn't hurt to go around by Main Street and then walk back.

And if she just happened to see Gus's truck, she just happened to see Gus's truck.

But she didn't see Gus's truck at all.

Of course he could have ridden in with someone else. She wasn't sure how she would really know if he was in there unless she went in herself.

No way was she going to do that!

But just as she was passing, a group of four cowboys, laughing and shoving each other, came out.

"Oh, hey!" one said. "How ya doin', Miz McLean?"

She recognized him from Thanksgiving dinner at Felicity and Taggart's. She smiled. "Fine. Just…fine. Out…taking a stroll. Got to get in my exercise every day, you know. For the baby."

All four cowboys gulped and nodded. "Yes, ma'am."

They shuffled back to give her a wide berth on the sidewalk, as if what she had might be contagious.

"Did, uh, Gus…come into town with you?" she asked. The words were out before she could stop them.

"No, ma'am," the tallest one said. "He went on up to Taggart's. Said he had to help Becky with her homework."

"Gus?" Mary had to work hard to keep her jaw from dragging on her toes.

"Yes, ma'am. Somethin' about a social studies project," said the shortest one.

"Well," she said. "Hmm," she said. She smiled vaguely

at the cowboys who bobbed their heads as she passed. "That's interesting."

It didn't make a whole lot of sense. But at least he wasn't in the Dew Drop—or anywhere else—socializing. And somehow that pleased her.

It shouldn't, she told herself.

But it did.

Sunday night Becky and Susannah relented and let him call her.

"You can ask her out," Susannah said.

"Out?"

"On a date," she explained patiently. "You're courting, remember?"

"Right." Gus scratched his head. Where the hell was he going to take her courting in Elmer?

"You don't have to take her to some place in Elmer," Becky said when he asked. "You could take her out to dinner in Livingston. Or to a movie."

"Or both," Susannah said magnanimously. "Go ahead and call her."

He called. He asked her out for Wednesday night. He refused to wait until Friday to see her again. He wanted Monday, but Susannah and Becky told him he couldn't, that he needed to give Mary at least a couple of days.

"Hey," he said when she answered. "It's me. I wondered if, um, maybe you'd like to go to dinner and see a movie? We could go over to Bozeman."

If he didn't take her that far away, he was afraid Becky and Susannah might find a ride into Livingston and stand there and watch to make sure he did it right.

"Wednesday? I can't, Gus," Mary apologized. "I just signed up for Lamaze childbirth classes at the hospital."

"You're taking a class to have a baby?" It sounded

weird to him, but other people thought going to school to learn how to ride a bronc was strange.

"It's about breathing techniques. Breath control and that sort of thing. So you're prepared when the time comes."

He thought fast. "How you gonna get there? I mean, if the roads are bad? I could drive you."

"Well, I—"

"I wouldn't mind. Really. What time does it start? Maybe we could have dinner first."

She hesitated again. Then, "Thank you," she said. "It starts at seven-thirty. That would be great."

They ate at a place Taggart recommended. A nice place with dark paneling and soft light that served good fish and even better steak.

Mary was surprised. "I thought you meant a burger place," she said when they went in.

"Why would you think that?"

"It's where we always went before."

"I told you," Gus said firmly, "things are different. Lots of things."

And he was determined she would know it.

He had no idea just how different things would be, though, until they'd finished eating and he took her to the hospital for her class.

"Where do you want me to wait?" The small reception area seemed full of people who were coughing, moaning or dripping blood. Gus had been in his share of hospital waiting rooms, but he'd always had a reason for being there.

He guessed he could go sit in the truck.

Mary regarded him for a moment, then got a wicked, challenging look in her eyes. "Well," she said, "I suppose you could always come along."

He gulped. "To your class?"

She smiled brightly. "Why not?"

Gus cocked his head and grinned. "Is this a dare, Mar'?" Dares from Mary were always interesting. One had got him a scar on his jaw, another the chip in his front tooth.

"Of course not." But her tone was just a little too bland.

"You think I won't do it. You think I'll turn tail and run." Gus could see it in her eyes. "Like hell," he said. "You're on."

She should have known better!

It wasn't enough that she'd practically dared Gus to come with her to the class, hoping, and failing, to discomfit him. Then she was discomfited herself when the instructor thought he was the dad!

Mary had met the instructor before. Her name was Cait Blasingame, and she worked with the doctor Mary had chosen to be her obstetrician. Cait was about Mary's age, though taller and considerably more slender—especially now. She had long brown hair that she wore in a braid down her back, and she was wearing jeans and a long-sleeved shirt that made her look more like a rancher than the nurse/midwife Mary knew she was.

The doctor had encouraged her to sign up for Cait's class, and when Mary had, they'd chatted for a few minutes, but they hadn't discussed the circumstances of Mary's pregnancy.

Apparently they should have.

"Listen, all you dads," Cait said briskly, eyes traveling from one nervous, awkward, get-me-out-of-here guy to another and, to Mary's horror, lingering on Gus, "you are very important to this process. Your part in this wasn't done six or seven or eight months ago. You don't get to go pace in the waiting room and let the little missus do all the work

No sir. You're going to be working right along with her. So let's get our jackets off and get ready to buckle down and get to work.''

Half a dozen men began shedding their jackets. So did Gus.

Drat him! Why didn't he just say he wasn't a father? Why didn't she?

Mary opened her mouth…but nothing came out.

"All right, now, ladies," Cait went on. "Let's stretch out on these mats on the floor. And fellas, you come kneel alongside."

Gus knelt beside her. Mary wanted to die.

"You don't have to," she hissed at him.

He grinned. "I want to."

"Well, I don't want you to!" She felt like a child in the middle of a squabble.

"Is there a problem?" Cait called from the front of the room.

"No problem," Gus said cheerfully, and his own grin dared Mary to contradict him.

Mary sighed. "No problem," she muttered.

Gus Holt wasn't the only one who could take a dare!

But if she thought stretching out in front of Gus's interested gaze was bad, things immediately got worse.

"All right, gents," Cait said briskly. "You can help best if you know how things feel. So I want each of you to put your hands on your lady's belly."

Gus needed no urging to do that. At once his hands spread against the curve of her abdomen.

Mary felt her face burn. She glared at him. He grinned back, unrepentant.

"I'm sure you all have a passing acquaintance with this new person who has come between you—" Cait grinned "—but I doubt if you've really taken the time to know what it's really like, minute by minute. So while I tell you what we're going to be doing over the next few weeks and show you a video of an actual birth, I want you to just leave your hands right there. I want you to feel the tension, the movement, the contractions if they happen. It won't be quite the same for you as it is for Mom, but I think it might open your eyes.''

It certainly opened Gus's.

Cait talked on, discussing the entire labor process, telling them what to expect, talking about how learning proper breathing techniques would help when the time came, how working with the contractions and learning to manage the discomfort could make the labor shorter and easier.

And all the time she talked, Gus's hands cupped Mary's abdomen. They felt the bump and grind of the small person who moved around inside. They jerked when they were kicked by the small person's foot. They flexed and rubbed almost unconsciously, it seemed to Mary, when her abdomen began to grow taut with one of the many light contractions she felt every day.

She didn't know if Gus heard a word Cait said. His attention seemed entirely focused on her belly. Mary had to admit to a certain distraction herself at the feel of strong masculine hands in such proximity. She could even get a little short of breath if she stopped to think that this was *Gus* who was holding her.

What if he thought she had known Cait was going to ask them to do this? The very notion made her cheeks burn. She actually broke out in a sweat, and her breathing grew quick and shallow.

''Are you okay?'' Gus bent close and spoke softly so only she could hear. He was so close his cheek brushed her hair.

Mary turned her head away "I'm fine. Of course I'm fine."

"You're sure?" He sat back on his haunches and lifted one hand from her belly to place it on her forehead. "You're hot."

"It's hot in here!" And getting hotter by the minute.

"You're right about that," Gus muttered, and Mary wondered if he was as flustered as she was.

"Okay, let's get comfortable now," Cait was saying as she put a video in the VCR. "Shift around, you fellows, and lean back against the wall so you can support your ladies."

The next thing Mary knew, Gus was seated against the wall and she was being tugged back to sit snug inside the V of his legs! His arms went around her and settled once more on her belly.

She felt the distinct urge to pant and it had nothing at all to do with the baby.

"The film is only twenty minutes. A very abbreviated labor. Don't go getting your hopes up." Cait laughed. "But it will give you some idea of what to expect. Keep your hands on your ladies, gentlemen." And she flipped off the lights and flicked on the video.

It was the longest—and shortest—twenty minutes Mary could remember. She didn't know how Cait expected her to pay attention to the screen. All she could think about was Gus—and not just about his hands on her abdomen now, but about his breath tickling her ear, about his thighs on either side of hers, about that part of him pressing firm and hard against her backside.

"Well," he murmured in her ear, "this is interesting." Something—his lips—his tongue—touched her ear.

She squirmed. "Gus!"

"Mmm." It was like a throaty tiger's purr in her ear. This time he nibbled. She squirmed again.

"If you think doing that is helping your cause, you're mistaken," Gus said wryly, and he pressed closer, making his point.

Literally, Mary thought, and stifled a sound that was half snort, half laughter.

Gus laughed, too, and his arms tightened around her. "Hold still." His voice was a caress against her ear. He gave her a tug to settle her against him and held her there.

Mary held still. She tried to focus on the video. Tried to forget Gus's arms, Gus's body, Gus himself wrapped around her.

"You can tune out distractions," she always told her kids in the classroom. "It's just a matter of willpower."

Sometimes, she realized, all the willpower in the world wasn't enough.

Finally, though, the video ended and Cait said, "Okay. Let's do a little practicing. Then you can work on it at home. That will be your homework this week. Ladies, flat-out. Deep breaths now. Really suck it in."

Mary looked at Gus. Gus looked at Mary. They both started to laugh. It was impossible not to.

"Ah, good. Here's a nice relaxed couple." Cait pounced on them. "Let's have you demonstrate."

"Oh, but—" Mary began.

But Cait had everyone gather round Gus and Mary and she taught them how Mary was supposed to breathe, how Gus was supposed to help her, support her, coach her.

"Wonderful," she said. "Excellent," she praised as Gus and Mary synchronized their breathing. She clapped Gus on the shoulder. "You're a natural."

"Oh, yeah," Gus muttered, and Mary was amazed to see a tide of red crawl up his neck and face.

*   *   *

"Of course you don't have to come back next week," Mary said the moment they were out the door. "I never meant for that to happen. I had no idea. I'm sorry. I never thought. Well, actually I thought you'd...you'd..."

Gus smiled and let her talk. They both knew what she'd thought. They both knew it wasn't what she'd got.

It was miles better, to Gus's way of thinking, though he had to admit to a certain amount of frustration that his body was just going to have to deal with.

He didn't imagine it was going to go away, either. But he didn't care. His body could deal with it.

He wasn't giving this up for anything.

"Don't get your hopes up, lady. I'm coming back next week."

"But—"

"I want to come, Mar'. I liked being there."

"Because we were...you were..." She looked down below his belt, then away again.

"That," he told her, "damn near drove me nuts."

"Well, that's why I said—"

"It's not just biology now, Mar'. I can live with it. I want to come back. I want to be there with you. I want to coach you."

Coaching her had been a kick. Of course, holding her had been wonderful. But having his hands on her, feeling the baby move and kick and stretch had been pretty amazing, too.

"Ruthie's going to coach me," Mary said. "When the time comes. She's taking a similar class."

"Sure. Fine. As long as I get to be there now."

"But why—"

"Because I love you, Mar'."

She was silent after that.

They were both silent all the way home.

He didn't know what she was thinking. She sat with her hands clasped and stared straight ahead. Gus gripped the steering wheel and told himself to keep his own mouth shut. He could think of a thousand things to say, to use, to try to convince her that he meant what he'd said.

But somehow he figured that maybe silence said it better. You couldn't argue someone into believing you loved them. You couldn't argue them into loving you.

He knew that.

But it was hard. God, it was hard!

He walked her to her door and, because now he knew Becky and Susannah were right, he forced himself not to ask to come in.

He said, "I know you must be tired."

"I am. Thank you for dinner. Thank you for...being there. I didn't mean..." Her voice trailed off again. She didn't look at him for a long moment. Then at last she did, and he saw that she looked worried, nervous, young and scared.

Gus wanted to make all those things go away. He wanted her to believe in him, to trust him. He wanted her to know that this time he'd be here for her.

But she didn't know it.

She wouldn't—unless he showed her. Proved it to her.

He touched her cheek. Then he leaned forward, dipped his head and touched his lips to hers. Just for a second, he told himself. Just a taste. Just a moment.

But the moment stretched to two. The kiss deepened. The ache of need inside him couldn't be assuaged with a mere brush of the lips, a gentle caress.

He needed—

But what mattered this time was what Mary needed.

He swallowed hard and, shuddering, pulled away. "Love

you,'' he said just a little unsteadily. ''I'll pick you up next Wednesday. We can have dinner again. Okay?''

Mary took a breath that seemed just a little tremulous, too. He saw her swallow. Then she nodded. ''Thanks, Gus.''

''My pleasure.'' Then he tugged down the brim of his hat and made himself turn and walk away.

Somehow Mary had been sure that pregnant women didn't have erotic dreams.

How could they, she'd reasoned, when their bodies were ungainly, misshapen things taken over by forces very much beyond their control?

Well, she'd been right about one thing—the force taking her over was very much out of her control.

She certainly didn't intend to toss and turn all night re-living the evening with Gus—and translating her body's urges into dreams that recalled vividly just what it had been like making love with Gus Holt.

Maybe it was because tonight's frustration reminded her all too much of the months she'd spent wanting Gus and denying him at the same time when they were teenagers. She'd valued the gift of her body too much to want to bestow it on just anyone. And even when she was sure she wanted to share it with Gus, she hadn't done it lightly.

She'd wanted to be sure they loved each other. She'd thought of it in terms of forever. She'd believed he did, too.

If she'd been wrong, it had been an honest mistake.

And if she'd been mistaken, the loving between them had been honest and true.

They were so young it had had to be. Neither of them had had the experience to pretend, to feign emotions or reactions they didn't feel.

She and Gus had loved each other with urgency and desperation and passion. They had loved each other with not only their bodies, but their hearts and souls.

For years Mary had tried to forget.

And she'd pretty much convinced herself she'd managed it. And then tonight, in the space of an hour, in every moment, in every touch, each and every memory came flooding back…

She'd gone with him to move cattle. It had been a warm June day. A perfect day—sunny with white clouds dancing lightly on the breeze. And while Gus had been working, Mary had just come along for the joy of being with him.

She'd packed a picnic lunch, which had amused Gus no end. But when they'd reached the field where he was to leave the cattle, there was a perfect rippling mountain stream and a flat rock alongside.

"A perfect place to have lunch," she'd said. And while Gus moved the cattle farther up the hillside, she'd waited there. She had spread out the thin cloth she'd brought along and had set out packets of sandwiches and chips. Then she'd settled down to wait for Gus to come back.

The sun had heated the rock beneath her, and she'd stretched out, enjoying the quiet, the gentle breeze, the soft white clouds in the blue sky overhead. Her summer job was at the public library where she cataloged books and dusted shelves. It was her day off—and a better vacation would have been hard to find. It was like being liberated, spending the day outside like this.

And then there was Gus.

She loved spending time with Gus. Riding with Gus. Talking with Gus. Dreaming with Gus.

She rolled over on the rock and watched him as he came toward her on horseback. She always marveled at the ease with which he moved, in complete concert with the animal.

She was a mediocre rider at best. But Gus...Gus was fantastic.

And he was hers.

She touched the ring on her finger. It was a narrow band of gold with a tiny chip of a diamond. But if it had been the Hope Diamond, it wouldn't have meant more. It was his pledge to her, his promise.

"I'll love you forever," he'd said when he'd given it to her only last week.

As she would love him.

He got off his horse, loosened the cinch and came toward her. Mary smiled, watching the rolling, loose-hipped, bow-legged way he walked.

She rolled up to a sitting position. "I have bologna sandwiches and peanut butter. Which do you want?" she asked.

"You," he said. "I want you."

His voice was just a little rough and ragged, and he ignored the sandwich she held out to him. Instead he dropped down beside her and took her in his arms.

He kissed her with a hunger that had nothing to do with how empty his stomach felt. This need went beyond that. It was bone deep, heart deep.

And Mary met it with a hunger of her own.

Always before, they'd stopped. They kissed, they'd touched, they'd caressed. He'd slid his hands up under her shirt or down the back of her jeans. She'd pressed her hips against the soft denim of his jeans and the hard flesh of his body. She'd felt his need.

And matched it with her own.

This time they didn't stop. When he opened the buttons to her shirt and unfastened the clasp of her bra, she didn't stop him. When he pressed hungry kisses on her breasts and fumbled with the zipper on her jeans, she didn't say no. She tugged his shirttails free and slid her hands up his back to stroke his fevered skin. She felt him shudder and saw the fine tremor of his fingers when he touched her waist to pull her jeans down.

The warm sun and the soft breeze caressed her heated flesh. But it didn't feel nearly as wonderful as Gus's fingers did. The skin was flushed and taut across his cheekbones as he wrestled with his own jeans. He muttered at his clumsiness.

"Here," she whispered. "Let me." She reached for him.

He shut his eyes, his jaw bunched. His whole body seemed to quiver. "No." The word came from between clenched teeth. "Don't. Touch."

"But—"

"Not. Now. Not. Yet." He was touching her, though. Brushing a hand over the hollow of her belly, over the tops of her thighs, over that very intimate part of her that so longed for him to touch it.

"Gus!" She didn't care what he said. If he could touch her, she could touch him. They were in this together. Forever. "Please!"

He'd freed himself from his jeans then, and she couldn't help but stare. She'd seen pictures, of course. She'd paid close attention when Mrs. Plum had hauled out all those clinical diagrams. But a diagram was a far cry from the real, hard, eager reality of Gus Holt.

Mary swallowed. Gus settled between her thighs. His fingers touched her, stroked her, made her crazy with longing for him. And so she reached for him.

"Mar'!" But he came to her, nudged her thighs wider, and together, awkwardly, fumblingly, they joined.

It was pain and it was pleasure. It was as if an emptiness she had never realized was filled—with love. With Gus.

He moved. A little. Trembled. A lot.

"I need— Oh, hell, Mar'! You need—!"

"You," she said. "I need you!" And she drew him down, her fingers clutching tightly into his muscular buttocks as she brought him home.

He bucked against her, his back arched, his eyes squeezed tightly shut. Then an almighty shudder ran through him and he went rigid. And Mary felt the warmth of his seed spill within her.

Gus's head dropped. His elbows bent. He settled onto her, into her, and rested his cheek against hers. "I love you," he whispered.

He'd whispered it every time they'd made love after that.

He'd been abashed and regretful that first time. "I was s'posed to make it good for you," he'd told her apologetically.

She'd touched his face. "It was good for me."

"You don't know," he'd insisted.

And he was right, she hadn't.

But in the coming months she'd found out. They'd learned together. He hadn't always been that urgent. He hadn't always been that frantic. He'd taken the time to meet her needs. He'd taken the time to help her find needs she hadn't even known she'd had! And then he'd met those. Willingly.

She'd tried not to think about that.

She'd tried not to miss it.

She'd lived without sex for a dozen years after Gus had broken their engagement. She didn't need it.

If she could survive without him, she'd assured herself, she could survive without sex.

And she had.

She still was.

But now she remembered what it had been like.

She remembered the closeness, the gentleness, the passion, the hunger. She remembered all of it.

Because Gus, damn it, was back in her life.

And she, fool that she was, had let him in. She'd gone to dinner with him. She'd gone to childbirth class with him.

Next thing you knew she'd be giving her heart to him.

No. Oh, no. Not again.

Memories were one thing. The future was something else.

Love was one thing.

Forever was another thing altogether.

Nine

So he was going to be seeing her every Wednesday night.

That was something.

It wasn't enough.

But he knew better now than to push. He knew he'd wormed his way as far as he dared into Mary's private life—for the moment at least.

Still, it was only one evening a week. He needed something else.

"Well, I suppose there's the Christmas pageant." Becky sounded doubtful.

"Christmas pageant?"

"We have one every year in Elmer. It's officially called The Winter Frolic now, but it's the Christmas pageant same as always," Susannah explained. "Carols. Musical numbers. Dancing. And of course the Nativity play. You know—" she shrugged "—just a Christmas pageant."

Gus hadn't been in a Christmas pageant since his mother

had twisted his ear and marched him into the Murray gymnasium and stuck a shepherd's crook in his hand. He had serious doubts about this one.

"Why would I want to get involved in a Christmas pageant?"

"Because Miz McLean's directing it," Becky told him. "Maybe you can be a wise man."

Not likely, Gus thought. "Okay, I'll go," he said. "But I don't think I'm gonna make it as a wise man."

"Don't worry," Becky said cheerfully. "Miz McLean will think of something. She always does."

Mary thought she was seeing things the next evening when Gus showed up at the Elmer Town Hall. She thought she was hearing things when he announced that he'd come to help out, to audition—he choked a little when he said that—to do whatever he could to help.

"Why?" she asked suspiciously. "Is this because of me?"

"You?" Gus blinked. "Well, yeah."

So at least he wasn't going to lie about it. Mary looked beyond him toward the group of shrieking, yelling fifth-graders that she was going to have to turn into something resembling a choir of angels in fifteen far-too-short minutes.

But then Gus added, "Partly, anyway. But since Taggart said I could work for him and that isn't really enough to make full-time, even with the road work, I've been talking to Jed McCall. I'm goin' to be workin' for him, too. So, as I'm for sure stickin' around, I figured I'd better start doin' my bit for the community."

Her jaw dropped. "You aren't serious."

"Course I am. I told you I was gonna work for Taggart. But I had to do some number crunchin', and when I did, I knew I'd need to line up somethin' else, too. I'd like to put somethin' down on a few acres of my own."

"Here?" She could feel her heart jamming its way into her throat.

"You're here."

"Gus, you can't be doing something like that because I'm here."

"Why not?"

Half a dozen interested children and adult volunteers looked equally interested in her answer to that question.

"You just *can't!*"

But before she could come up with any better reason than that, Alice Benn bustled over. "Ah, Gus, dear. How sweet of you to come! Isn't this a treat? We don't have a Joseph yet."

"No!" Gus blurted at the same time Mary said, "Oh, no."

Alice's eyes grew wide as dinner plates. "No? But it's such a perfect part. He can play opposite you, Mary, and—"

"No!" Mary said firmly. It was bad enough he was coming to childbirth classes with her. She did not need him acting the part of Joseph in the pageant, especially not after she'd been shanghaied into playing Mary because Poppy was too close to delivery to hope she'd make it until Christmas week, and no one else wanted to stuff a pillow under her bathrobe to accomplish what Mary could just by being there.

"You're Mary?" Gus's brows hiked up. He looked as if he were reconsidering.

"That's my name."

"Well, I think it's a perfect idea," Alice gushed.

"Gus can't act," Mary said flatly.

"Well, I—"

"No!"

But she'd have to come up with something. He wasn't just going to walk away. She'd seen that light in his eyes before. She'd have to find him a job that kept him busy and away—far away—from her.

The door to the hall opened and Tuck McCall shouted, "Where d'you want the rabbits, Miz McLean?"

"Rabbits?" Gus said.

Mary smiled. She laughed. She beamed. "Gus will take them," she called back.

Gus stared at her, stupefied.

"You can be the bunny wrangler!" Mary told him.

The bunny wrangler.

"You take care of livestock, don't you?" she'd said when he'd opened his mouth to protest. "Well, it's right up your alley, then. You wanted to help. You can take care of the livestock. In this case, the livestock are bunnies."

"Whoever heard of bunnies at Christmas?" Gus demanded.

"We don't have room for sheep in the hall," Mary explained practically. "But the children like real animals. They're interesting. They add an aura of authenticity. And you did say you wanted to help?" The look she gave him dared him—just as he'd known it would.

Gus herded bunnies.

That meant seeing that they were onstage when required and shuffled neatly off to their cages when they were not. It meant cleaning up after the critters when they did things that no self-respecting actor should do while onstage. It meant having half a hundred kindergartners crawling all over him wanting to help him while he did his job. It meant showing each and every one of them how to hold a rabbit gently, to stroke it softly and not—for Pete's sake!—to let it go so that it skittered under the stage or behind the curtain or beneath that huge stack of folding chairs that would fall and crush it if he weren't absolutely careful trying to catch it again.

He did it all without complaint.

But he told Mary with his eyes that she wasn't going to get away with it. That there would be a time—and a place—for them.

But Mary, it seemed, stayed one step ahead.

She was Mary in the Nativity play one minute. She was the director of the angel's choir the next. She coached the shepherds to look awestruck and the wise men not to trip over their robes. She took on the unenviable task of choosing a baby Jesus from the babies who auditioned. And she managed not to offend any of their mothers—a major miracle as far as Gus could see.

Every minute she kept working. She had vision. Ideas. She drew word pictures to set the scene and before long had everyone clamoring to create what she suggested.

"A rustic crib," she thought aloud. "And a roughed-in sort of wooden manger. Not much, but it will seem much more real to the children. If only..." She looked hopeful.

"I'll build you a crib...and a manger," Gus said.

He did. When he wasn't wrangling bunnies, he was sawing wood, hammering nails, putting up sets. And out of the corner of his eye he was watching Mary as she bustled from one project to the next, encouraging, helping, laughing, supporting.

He was aware of when all was going well, and he noticed when she stopped and rubbed at her back as if it was bothering her. Then he set down his hammer and crossed the set, coming up behind her silently and beginning to rub her back.

She jumped, startled. Then she made a soft sound, somewhere between a whimper and a moan.

"You should sit down," Gus's hands worked rhythmically over the tight bands of muscle in her lower back, then worked their way up her spine and down again.

"Can't," Mary breathed. "I'd fall asleep if I did." It was late and she'd put in a full day at school.

"You don't need to do this."

"Of course I do!"

"Not all of it. They expected a simple Christmas pageant. You didn't, for example, have to give them the Rockettes."

That was the group of elementary-aged girls who had come in last week just desperately wanting to do a dance number—if only Mary would coach them.

"This is a Christmas play," he reminded her, still kneading, loving the way she arched her back and almost purred in response.

"It's a community celebration," she corrected. "It's evolving."

"I'll say," he muttered.

Over the past week he'd built a crib and a manger—and the set for an entire row of storefronts for one of the musical production numbers.

He hadn't believed it when he'd heard her say, "Production numbers," the first time. He'd stared at her, then had dared to ask, "Are you out of your mind?"

"We can't just do a Nativity scene and the traditional Biblical story. There's too much congestion at the manger."

He laughed.

But she went on quite seriously. "We have to have other scenes to accommodate everyone who wants to have a part.

All ages. That's why we're doing 'Silver Bells,' 'Winter Wonderland,' 'Frosty the Snowman.'"

"I don't believe this," he fumed to Becky the next morning.

"Oh, it's normal," Becky said. "I was an auxiliary snow person once."

Gus was clearly out of his depth.

But he didn't give up. If he wanted to prove anything to Mary, he couldn't.

So he herded the damn bunnies. He built the damn sets. He showed up every day after he finished helping Taggart and Noah. He made it a point to pick Mary up at school and take her out to dinner before they went to the town hall or, if he took her home, he cooked for her there.

"You don't have to do this," she told him every day.

He ignored her. It wasn't true. He did have to do it. For her. For himself.

She kept protesting. But she stopped fighting.

He took her to every Lamaze class. They didn't even discuss it. He picked her up and took her down to Livingston for dinner. Then they went to class together. It was a given.

They were a couple.

Gus was delighted, convinced he was wearing her down.

He was wearing her down.

The only thing Mary could hope was that all this exposure to bunnies and babies, an angel's choir that preferred shooting hoops to singing hallelujahs, not to mention three vertically challenged wise men who kept falling over their fathers' bathrobes and a couple of retired teachers with matchmaking on their minds was wearing Gus down, too.

Norman Rockwell Does Montana wasn't Gus's scene. She was sure of it.

Gus liked moving on. Gus liked going down the road.

He would be heading down this road anyday now, Mary was sure of it. No matter what he said.

But day after day, contrary to all her hopes and expectations, Gus stuck around.

He showed up at school and insisted on taking her to dinner or, when she declined that, on coming back to her place and cooking for her there.

She let him do it at first because she intended to call his bluff. She didn't think he could cook.

He wasn't a cordon bleu chef by any means. But he could put a well-balanced meal on the table. He even cited some nutritional study on the dietary needs of pregnant women that he'd asked Cait to give him to read. He even stood over her, making sure she drank all her milk!

Mary didn't encourage him. On the contrary she sometimes graded papers right through the meal. She wasn't deliberately trying to be rude. She was just under a lot of pressure to get both the pageant and her classroom work done.

Gus said he understood. And he persevered.

He took care of the bunnies. He said terrible things about them, calling them Lunch and Stew and Fricassee and Giblets and promising them dire consequences after their fifteen minutes of fame.

But he was always right there with them whenever they were needed, and he was careful to make sure no child held one too tightly. More than once Mary found him showing a child how to hold a bunny so that both the bunny and the child lived to tell about it.

She was struck by his gentleness. The first time she saw him hunkered down, a child and a bunny in his lap, she was entranced. And she would have stood right there and watched, but he'd looked up then and when he saw her he'd winked.

She'd turned back to her own work immediately, but the image stayed with her.

So did Gus.

Wherever she was in the hall—working with the "Frosty the Snowman" troupe, playing Mary in the Nativity sequence, rehearsing the hyperactive angels' choir, or trying to hang lights from the town hall Christmas tree, Gus was there, too.

He always seemed to be the one to hand her the props she needed or to take the Christmas lights out of her hand and lift her off the ladder and say, "I'll do that."

He was the one who mopped up wise man Frankie Setsma's bloody nose when the boy's father's bathrobe tripped him up and sent him sprawling into the side of the manger.

He got the angelic choir to settle down and sing, which was more than she managed sometimes.

She was good with kids, but she was low on energy. She needed help. Gus gave it. That was that.

He ran the show with the ease and competence of a five-star general. It surprised her. Gus had always seemed so laid-back and mellow. Now he was organized and efficient. She half expected the kids to be saluting and saying, "Sir! Yes, sir!" as they jumped to obey his commands.

She had created a monster.

Or so she told herself.

But then, one night after everyone else had left, when Mary finally finished working and everything was completely quiet and she thought even Gus was long gone, she found him sitting on the floor backstage.

Stew-the-bunny was snuggled on his lap, and he was

scratching the bunny's ears. He looked up at her when she appeared from behind the set.

"You softie," Mary chided, her heart feeling strangely large in her chest.

Gus gave her one of his heart-stopping, lopsided grins—the ones that had been able to melt her since junior high school—and winked. "Don't tell."

"No," she said. She tried to sound matter-of-fact, but her voice came out sounding rusty, as if she hadn't used it in a while. It was really, she assured herself, that she'd been using it all too much tonight.

"Ready to go?" Gus got to his feet, still cradling Stew gently in his hands.

"I'm finished. But you don't have to come with me."

Gus put Stew in his cage, then he checked the rabbit's water and food. "I thought we'd settled that."

"I don't expect—"

He latched Stew's catch, then turned and caught her by the arms.

"Gus!" She protested.

But inexorably, he pulled her closer, until her ballooning belly rested hard against his. Then he leaned forward and touched her lips with his. Firmly. Possessively.

"Expect," he said. Then he kissed her—really kissed her this time—long and hard.

She dreamed about him that night.

It was the kiss that caused it. It was the kiss that reminded her of what she'd been trying so hard to forget—the physical side of loving Gus.

Their close encounters at her class on Wednesday nights brought the memories back. Gus's presence at the town hall kept them simmering.

But that kiss had been like dumping gasoline on a smoldering ember.

In her dreams she made love with Gus.

And this Gus wasn't the nineteen-year-old boy she'd been engaged to, he wasn't the teenager she'd loved in the flesh. This Gus—the Gus of her dreams—was the man he'd become.

He was the man who'd held Stew so gently and had taught countless kindergartners how to hold him as well. He was the man who had wiped Frankie's nose and who had felt her contractions and who had cooked her supper.

He was the man who had kissed her senseless tonight.

It was a memorable dream. A scary dream. What had become of her determined indifference?

She sat on the bed, trying to hug her knees, but the baby was too big, and she couldn't wrap her arms around her knees anymore, no matter how much she tried.

The baby shifted and stretched. It bumped and elbowed her. Trying to get more room, no doubt. "Poor thing," she said and patted her belly. "Not long now. Two more months and you'll have lots of room to stretch."

The minute she said the words, she wished she hadn't.

It was the one thing—besides Gus—that she really didn't want to think about: what she would do when the baby was gone.

Her doctor said she needed to consider it, needed to be ready for it.

"It will be a little like a death for you," he'd told her frankly. "You won't be going home with a baby. Your sister will."

"I always knew that," Mary had replied. She said it to herself again now. But saying it didn't stop the hollow feeling she got when she dwelt on it.

"So stop dwelling on it," she muttered. "Get up and get moving. Time to get to work."

She went to work. She taught her classes. Tonight there was no rehearsal because it was Wednesday, the night for her childbirth class.

Mary didn't know if she could take another one. Not after the dream she'd had last night!

Maybe, she thought, Gus wouldn't come.

Yeah, right.

He was there waiting by the door when she came out of school. It had been a sunny day and not especially cold. "I don't need a ride," she told him.

"And hello to you, too." He grinned at her, then leaned forward, angled around her belly and dropped a kiss on her lips.

"Gus!"

"What?" His look was pure innocence.

"We're in the middle of a public place!"

"And that's as far as it will go—here. I promise." He crossed his heart, still grinning.

"I don't know why you're doing this," she grumbled. "What do you want?"

He took her arm and led her across the street toward his truck. "You know what I want. You."

"For the moment," she conceded. "But you won't want me forever."

"Yes," Gus said firmly. "I will." He put his hand on the truck door, holding it shut, trapping her between him and the door. "I am grown-up now, Mar'. I know you don't trust me yet. I'm tryin' to help you learn to trust me. Give me a chance."

She turned her head away so she didn't have to look into the jade green depths of his eyes. But he touched her cheek

with a finger and turned her head so that she had to meet
his gaze.

"Give me a chance, Mar'," he repeated.

She swallowed. She blinked.

"Please."

She shrugged, annoyed at him for pushing her, annoyed
at herself for letting him.

Gus brushed a hand over her hair, then kissed her lightly
once more. "That's my girl."

This Wednesday night was no easier than the others.

Gus got to put his hands all over her—and he couldn't
do a thing. It drove him nuts. It made him horny as hell.

She made him horny as hell. But when he said she was
driving him crazy, she didn't believe a word of it.

They were in the parking lot after the class and he kept
losing track of the conversation because, like any guy
who'd just had his hands all over the woman he loved for
an hour, Gus wasn't thinking about whether the snowman
in the "Frosty" scene needed a top hat or if his father's
cowboy hat would do.

"Huh?" he said for what had to be the fifth or sixth
time.

"Are you listening, Gus? What's the matter with you?"

"I want you." There it was, stark and simple. Right out
there between them as they stood in the light of the parking
lot.

"You *want* me? *Me?*" Mary looked at him, then down
at her fairly enormous belly, then back up at him in dis-
belief. "You can't."

He hauled her sideways against him so she could tell just
exactly what he meant.

"Oh. Oh, my." Her eyes were like saucers as she looked
at him again. The color rose in her cheeks. He could see it

even in the dim light of the parking lot. She gave a little shake. "You're oversexed," she told him primly.

He laughed. "No. I'm underprivileged."

"Well, there are a lot of other women in the world," she reminded him huffily.

"No," Gus said. "There's only you."

He guessed it was his penance, having to fight his way back to having what he'd so blithely tossed away years ago. It served him right; he'd be the first to admit it.

But this was taking forever.

Mary was right—he'd never been a forever kind of guy. He was having to learn.

He was determined he would.

Mary seemed just as determined that he wouldn't.

"I don't know how you can find me sexy," she said when they were headed back to Elmer.

Gus didn't think that was worth a reply. A guy would have to be dead not to find Mary sexy.

"Most men don't," she went on.

"Did you take a survey?"

"I didn't have to. Matt—the guy I was dating last summer when I got pregnant in the first place—was totally turned off."

"Matt was an idiot."

"He didn't like the idea of me being pregnant with another man's child."

"That's his problem, not yours."

"People think it's weird."

Gus scratched the back of his head. "I have to admit, it made me stop and think, that's for sure. But not about you carrying someone else's baby. I was wondering if you belonged to someone else, too. Once I found out you didn't, I thought it was great. In fact—" he shot her a grin "—I think it's a hell of a nice thing to do."

"It's not that simple," Mary argued. "It's complicated."

"Not to me. It's a gift, what you're doing. Helluva gift if you ask me." He reached over and took her hand and squeezed it gently. Then he hung on, curved his fingers around hers and tucked them against his thigh.

"Don't do this, Gus," she begged.

"Don't do what?"

"Don't be so nice. Don't make me fall in love with you again."

"I want you to, hon'."

She shook her head silently, determinedly. But she didn't try to pull her hand away.

Come on, Mar'. Love me. Trust me. Please. But Gus didn't say the words aloud. He'd said them already and she'd resisted, turning a deaf ear.

This time he said them silently—and hoped she would hear them in her heart.

Two wise men got the chicken pox on Thursday.

Fricassee had babies—five of them!—on Friday.

One of the angel choir broke his arm on Saturday.

It had snowed eighteen inches by Sunday morning.

And on Sunday afternoon, just hours before the pageant was to begin, Shane, who had been drafted to be Joseph, called to say he was taking Poppy to the hospital in labor.

"Ah, well," Cloris said as they gathered at the town hall that night. "We shall endure. The show must go on!"

"But who else knows the lines?" Alice fretted. Angels were beginning to arrive. Frosty was looking for his dad's cowboy hat, worried that they might have left it at home.

"Gus does," Cloris said.

She looked at Gus. Becky looked at Gus. Everyone looked at Gus.

And then at Mary.

"There aren't that many lines," Mary said testily. She did *not* want Gus playing Joseph. "He only has to murmur sympathetic things and ask if there's room at the inn. Get your dad," she said to Becky. "He can do it. We need Gus to take care of the bunnies."

"But—" Becky began.

"Get your dad!" Mary snapped. Then she shut her eyes and prayed for strength and calm and for her back to stop aching.

It had been nagging her all day. Finally she opened her eyes again.

"I'm sorry," she said to Becky who was regarding her worriedly. "I'm just a little…tired. Could you please ask your father if he'll do it? I really need…Gus to do other things."

That much was true. It wasn't just that she didn't want to play opposite Gus. It was also that she needed Gus to keep everything else running smoothly.

Gus was the only one who could quell the angels with a look. He was the only one who could keep track of the rabbits and the cowboy hats, and the only one who seemed to make everyone do what they were supposed to do so that she could direct.

"I'll get my dad," Becky said.

Mary smiled tightly. "Thank you." She rolled her shoulders, trying to ease the tension in them. "All right, everybody. Let's get in your places."

"You okay?" Gus asked her while everyone else was scrambling to be wherever they belonged.

"Fine," Mary said absently. "Can you keep an eye on the angels. I don't need any blood flowing before they sing."

"I'll keep an eye on the angels."

"I don't know why I agreed to do this," Mary mumbled.

At least the baby wasn't kicking her today. It had been very quiet, which was a good thing, because between her back and the tightness in her shoulders and, every once in a while, across her abdomen, she had all she could deal with right now. She gave her belly a little pat.

"You're being very good," she told the baby inside. "Think valentines. It won't be long now."

Somewhere between "Frosty the Snowman" and "Silver Bells" she began to realize how right she was.

The tightening across her abdomen became rhythmic, surprisingly strong and getting stronger all the time. Periodically Mary pressed a hand against her belly and tried to shift things, to perhaps hint to the baby that now was not the time to be trying to stretch its quarters.

The tightening eased. She relaxed.

She went into the single tiny restroom to don her Mary garb, then arranged the shawl and checked herself in the mirror. Talk about type casting. She looked as big as a house.

There was a frantic banging on the door. "Miz McLean! I gotta pee!" It was Frankie Setsma. "It's urgent," he muttered when she opened the door. He dashed past her into the bathroom.

She shook her head and started backstage when the tightening began again. Harder. Stronger. Firmer. She pressed her hand on her belly.

"Don't," she commanded it. "It's too soon. Too early. Not now."

The angels were bumping and thumping their way onto the stage to be the backup chorus for the Nativity. At least there was no blood yet, though they were getting restless and nervous, a deadly combination.

Frankie came back, struggling into the bathrobe his

mother had hemmed so he wouldn't trip over it this evening.

"Ready?" Mary asked.

"What if I have to pee again?"

"You just did." Gus appeared holding Stew and Lunch.
He handed them to Frankie.

"But what if I have to again?"

"It's just stage fright, Frankie," Mary said just as a contraction hit her. She wasn't prepared this time, and it came
faster and fiercer than the earlier ones. It made her gasp.

"What's wrong?" Gus demanded.

"N-nothing." Mary smoothed the long dress and shawl
over her abdomen, gritting her teeth as the pain passed.
"Nothing's wrong." But for the first time she thought this
wasn't just a dress rehearsal.

Gus looked at her gravely, then narrowly. He laid a hand
next to hers. She tried to swat it away, but even though
Frankie's eyes grew round and wondering, Gus held firm.

"How long?" he demanded after a moment.

Mary shrugged. "A while."

"Strong?"

"A little."

"How little?"

She hesitated. "Not very. They're...stronger than I've
ever had them," she admitted.

His jaw tightened. "How far apart?"

"I haven't timed them."

"Mar'!"

"When have I had time to time them?"

Gus pushed back his sleeve and glanced at his watch.
"Okay. Tell me when the next one hits. Go sit down."

"I can't go sit down! I have to be ready to go on."

Even as she spoke, she could hear Polly McMaster, the
postmistress, who was the narrator of the piece begin to

read the Christmas story. "And you can't stand here staring at your watch. You have to get the rest of the bunnies!"

Gus said something very rude about the bunnies.

Frankie looked shocked.

Mary kicked Gus's shin. "Go get Giblets and the rest of them. You've got to get the donkey, too. Stop worrying about me."

The donkey was a show time addition. He'd never been to rehearsal, but Taggart had assured her that he would do his part without it.

"We've got one donkey already," Gus muttered now. "The real one's got nothin' on you. Stubborn woman." He peeled off his watch and handed it to her. "Time them." He strode off.

In a minute he was back. He gave the other shepherds the rest of the rabbits, then went out and came back with the donkey.

Taggart appeared in something that looked like one of Cloris's tablecloths. "Shane took his costume with him," he muttered. "It's all there was."

He moved to boost Mary up onto the donkey's back, but Gus thrust the donkey's lead into his hand instead.

"I'll do that."

And the next thing Mary knew, Gus had lifted her onto the donkey. She wobbled. She felt another contraction begin.

"Ready?" Taggart asked.

Mary clutched at the donkey's back, but there was nothing to hold on to. Gus was still holding her. And she gripped his hands in her own, grateful to have him there for once.

"How far apart?" Gus demanded.

"What?" Taggart looked aghast.

"Four minutes," Mary said.

"...a decree was issued by the Emperor Augustus for a registration to be made," Polly was intoning.

"That's us," Mary said. "Go."

Taggart stared at her, stupefied.

"Go on!" she urged him. "The quicker the better."

Something about her look or tone galvanized him. "Right!" He tugged the donkey forward. It jolted and shuffled along after him. On its back, Mary shut her eyes and prayed.

She didn't even realize she was still clutching Gus's hand until everyone in the audience started to murmur. Then her eyes jerked open and she saw Gus standing right behind her, grimly hanging on.

Taggart went straight to the inn and banged on the door. It opened.

Otis Jameson poked his head out. "No room!" he growled, and shut it again.

Taggart started to knock again when Gus said, "Damn it, she's going to have this baby. Hurry up and get this over with!"

As a showstopper, that was all it took.

Ten

She wasn't having the baby.

Not now! Not yet!

She *couldn't* be having the baby!

It wasn't due for six and a half weeks. Not until Valentine's Day.

It was the stress. Mary knew she had been working too hard. Thinking about the pageant, about the songs, the plays, the kids, the livestock.

About Gus.

She shot him a quick glance now as he drove hell-for-leather for Livingston. From the grim set of his mouth, she knew he was worried, too.

"I'm not having it," she said, though whether to reassure him or herself, she wasn't sure.

He reached out a hand and without even glancing her way, took hers unerringly in his. He gave it a squeeze. "I damned well hope not," he said roughly.

"If I do—" her voice wavered "—if I do...do you th-think I might l-lose it."

"You're not gonna lose it." His voice was gruff and hard and firm, and he flicked her a quick glance. "You won't lose it," he promised. "We won't let it happen."

She didn't know why now, of all times, she believed him. But the sheer force of his determination buoyed her weary spirit. She clung to his hand.

"No," she whispered. "We won't."

Gus hoped to God she believed him. He wasn't sure he believed himself.

He wasn't nearly as confident as he tried to sound.

What the hell did he know about having a baby?

He'd played midwife to a few mamma cows over the years, but it could hardly compare. You didn't have to help them with their breathing. And they didn't hang on to your hand as if you were a lifeline.

Oh, wow, Gus thought. Oh, God. Oh, wow.

Felicity had called the hospital to let them know Mary was on her way. Thank heavens the doctor was already there when they arrived.

So was Cait. She gave Mary a hug and a smile and a thumbs-up sign. She took Gus by the arm.

"I'm just going to show him where to sign in," she told Mary, "and I'll be right back."

When she had him around the corner her smile faded. "What happened? How long has it been going on?"

He tried to tell her. He tried to remember all the stuff she'd told them during class to notice. He relayed it as best he could.

Cait listened. She nodded. She knew about Mary's circumstances now, knew this wasn't your run-of-the-mill pregnancy. Mary had told her after the first class.

She knew Gus wasn't the father, but she seemed to understand that he needed to be there.

"Okay, then." Cait squeezed his hand and her soft-blue eyes met his. "You ready?"

Gus cleared his throat, then nodded. "As I'll ever be, I guess."

She gave him a grin. "That's the spirit. You just keep her going. We're not going to let anything happen to this little one." She gave his arm a squeeze. "Or Mary."

He was a rock.

Her rock.

Steady. Solid. Unflappable. Cool. Calm. Grace under pressure.

That was Gus.

"Steady now. Ride it out. Easy, easy. Breathe with me." He locked his hands with hers as he locked his eyes with hers. It was as if there was no one else in the world.

No doctor saying, "Right, right. Just hold it now." Then, "Okay, pant. Pant. Now push. That's it. Push!"

No Cait saying, "You're doing fine, Mary. That's a girl. Steady, steady. That's it. You're doing it."

Mary knew she wasn't doing it. Not alone. Gus was doing it with her.

That's how it felt. As if she had locked onto him. As if she could hear only him. Respond to only him.

He was her strength. She hung on to his hands, she gripped his wrists. She might have snapped them right in two at the last when the baby finally pushed its way into the world.

She sagged back and heard a whimper, a tiny cry. Frail. Then stronger. Lustier.

"It's a boy!" the doctor said.

And Mary and Gus looked at each other and wept—and grinned.

All Gus could think was, it was a good thing it had just happened—slap, bang—one minute he was holding Mary on a donkey and the next he was shooting down the road as if a mad bull was after him, and the next he was holding on to her for dear life while she gave birth to this child.

This child.

It was here. Now.

Alive and well.

He looked at the tiny baby swaddled in a soft blue blanket and nestled in Mary's arms, and he could hardly believe it was real—*he* was real.

Sure he'd felt the baby move. Intellectually he had always known that inside Mary there was this...this *person*...just biding its time, growing strong enough to meet the world on its own terms.

But he was so tiny, this person. So incredibly small. And so perfect.

Such a perfect child.

"He is a gift," Gus said gruffly, his throat tight.

The whole thing was a gift as far as he was concerned. Not only the baby, but Gus's being allowed to be here, to share in this, was a gift—one he had no right to, had certainly never hoped for, could not have expected.

Gus had never felt very humble. He felt humble now.

Mary stroked the baby's soft, peach-colored fuzz that someday might be a head of hair. "He is," she agreed softly. "Jonathan."

That was the name Ruthie and Jeff had picked.

"That's what it means—God's gift," she told Gus, eyes shining.

"Kid's got a name longer than he is," Gus said softly.

He stood up and moved to stand beside the bed, to look down on them both. He bent his head and dropped a kiss on her forehead. "Should've named him Mary's Gift."

Mary gave him a watery smile. "He'd get teased on the schoolyard, that's for sure."

"He could go by his initials. Nothing wrong with M.G. He could tell 'em he was named for a car."

"Like you?"

Gus grimaced. "I wasn't named for a car."

"I didn't think you were." She'd figured out pretty quickly that his middle name was Augustus. It was the first name he couldn't bring himself to tell her.

"Not Dodge? Not Daimler?" she teased.

He shook his head.

"Are you ever going to tell me?"

"If you'll marry me." The words came out without him even thinking.

And it was as if the world had come to a stop.

Mary stared at him. She looked confused. And shocked.

And Gus, knowing he had said them at the wrong time and far too soon, could hardly retract them now. He had to press on.

"You know I want to marry you. I've told you I love you. I always have. I just didn't always know what it meant. I admit I'm a little slow. Well, maybe I'm a lot slow. But when I figure something out, I've got it for good. I've got this, Mar'. Do you believe me?"

She didn't answer. Her throat worked and she blinked rapidly. Her lips trembled and she bent her head, so that her gaze was on the baby not on him.

No answer was an answer. And though he didn't want to, Gus heard it very well.

His gut twisted. He swallowed hard.

"It's okay. I understand." He forced the words past the

lump in his throat. He reached out a hand and brushed it lightly over her hair. "Rest," he told her. "Get some sleep. You've had a hard day."

Heart breaking, he turned and walked slowly out the door.

She wanted to say yes.

Mary knew as she watched him walk away that she wanted to marry Gus Holt. Wanted them to be together forever. She wanted to call him back. But she couldn't.

She clutched Jonathan close against her and blinked as the tears brimmed, then slid silently down her cheeks.

She couldn't offer him her heart. She'd done it once.

And if he'd changed, she had, too. She wasn't young and trusting anymore. She wasn't innocent.

She was afraid.

It was the best Christmas ever.

Ruthie said so. So did Jeff.

They brought Jonathan home from the hospital to Mary's house on Christmas morning, and they were all there together, snug and warm and joyful.

"A family," Ruthie said. "At last."

They were. And Mary was a part of it, too, of course. An important part.

But not an integral part.

The day after tomorrow Ruthie and Jeff and Jonathan would be flying home to Phoenix—and Mary would have her life back.

Sort of.

She would be fine, she assured herself.

She had a circle of friends here now, a core of loving, caring people who would be her family. She had Alice and Cloris. She had Felicity and Taggart and Becky and the

ANNE McALLISTER 171

twins. She had Jenny and Mace Nichols and their family. She had Shane and Poppy and their new baby daughter, Hannah, who had been born just a few hours before Jonathan. She had Jed and Brenna McCall and their bunch. She had a new friend in Cait.

Cait would be someone to share a video with on a Saturday night. Someone to drive over to Bozeman with to catch a movie. Someone—because Cait lived on a ranch—to lend her a horse to ride up into the hills where she would be able to look out across the valley and the mountains and tell herself she had many blessings, that she ought to be content.

Mary was determined to be content.

She would not miss Gus.

It always came back to Gus.

She didn't mention Gus to Ruthie and Jeff other than to say he'd been the one to help her through her labor. She didn't tell them he'd asked her to marry him just scant hours later.

She didn't think about it. It hurt too much.

She expected he would come along with the hordes of well-wishers who came on Christmas and the day after to visit Jonathan and his parents before they went home to Arizona.

Half the valley, it seemed, dropped in.

Cloris and Alice and several of the townspeople came Christmas afternoon. But Gus never appeared.

The day after Christmas all the Joneses came, even Will and Gaye from Bozeman. So did all the Nicholses—including Poppy and brand-new baby Hannah, who was very nearly as precious as Jonathan and, according to her father, promised to be a pistol. Shane said he was already quaking in his boots.

"You notice," he said, puffed with fatherly pride, "that she has her mama's red hair."

Mary noticed. She noticed everything. The babies. The children. The couples. The warmth, the love, the caring that existed between them.

Mostly she noticed that Gus wasn't there.

She wanted to ask Becky where he was, but she couldn't seem to say his name. She couldn't ask. She'd wait. Sooner or later someone would mention him. How could they not talk about Gus?

People did talk about Gus.

They talked about how much he'd done on the pageant, how funny he'd been with the rabbits, how hard he'd worked building the manger, how attentive he'd been to Mary.

Taggart told Ruthie how Gus had come right onstage with Mary in the Nativity play. "First time Mary ever had a bodyguard!" He laughed.

Everyone else laughed, too.

Jeff said, "He was there when he needed to be, that's for sure. I was glad I got to thank him."

Mary straightened. When? When had Jeff seen him? When had Jeff thanked him?

Ruthie nodded, cuddling Jonathan close, as she answered Mary's unspoken question. "He came by the hospital early Christmas morning and brought Jonathan this."

She reached down, fumbled through the piles of baby gifts and Christmas presents and came up with a fluffy, stuffed black-and-white bunny who looked remarkably like Stew.

"He said Jonathan should have one as a souvenir." Ruthie giggled and everyone else grinned.

Mary smiled, too, and swallowed hard. She took the rabbit when Ruthie looked for somewhere to put it down again.

She cradled it in her arms and let everyone's happiness and laughter and joy wash over her.

She wished they would all go home and leave her alone to pull the covers over her head.

"You're a hero," Becky told him.

"Everybody says so," Susannah concurred.

"They've got a pretty feeble grasp of heroism," Gus muttered.

He was clearing out the drawers of the dresser he'd used, tossing his clothes in his duffel bag, wishing Becky and Susannah would just go away.

"You helped Jonathan get born," Becky persisted. "You got Miz McLean to the hospital and stayed with her and coached her an' everything. Doc Ryan says that without you things might not have gone so well."

"Cait says you were fantastic," Susannah put in.

Gus noticed they weren't quoting Mary. He figured Mary had had nothing to say. He shrugged. "I did what needed to be done. No big deal. Anybody would have." Which was nothing but the truth.

"Well, anybody didn't," Becky said indignantly. "You did! So why are you packin'? Why didn't you come with us to see them yesterday? They're gone now with the baby. But Miz McLean's still there. You're goin' to see her, aren't you? Gus!" she said urgently, finally looking around and noticing that he'd stuck everything in his bag. "How come you're packin'? What's the matter with you?"

He was through. Finished. Done for.

He had no hopes left.

He'd rushed his fences, had asked too soon. Or maybe rushing his proposal hadn't made any difference at all. Maybe she would have said no if he'd waited a month, a year, a lifetime. Maybe this had just ended things quicker.

Maybe Mary would never trust him again, no matter what.

Not enough to risk marrying him, anyway.

Maybe you got just one shot at a thing like that. And if you blew it…well, you blew it. Gus understood that. It was like ridin' a bronc. You missed him out of the chute or got bucked off along the way, too damn bad. You didn't win the buckle.

He hadn't won the buckle.

And unlike rodeo, there were no rerides in life.

He finished stuffing his gear in his duffel and zipped it up. Then he turned to the girls who were sitting on his bunk, and he explained. He forced himself to say the words he'd hoped he would never have to say.

"I told you I hurt her a long time ago. We were going to get married and I backed out. Just called her up and said I couldn't go through with it. I couldn't face settlin' down. She loved me then, and I loved her. But I still couldn't do it." He rubbed a hand over his hair. "I didn't realize what I was givin' away."

They sat in silence, watching him pace around the room. He didn't want to talk about it at all, but he'd asked for their help. They'd given it. And it wasn't their fault it hadn't worked. He wanted to be sure they knew that.

"It was my fault. You guys tried to help. But it was too late. It's always been too late. I'd give anything to do it all over again—but it doesn't work that way. You can't go back."

"But—"

He shook his head. "You can't." He smiled at the irony of it. "It serves me right. Mary doesn't want me now. And who can blame her? I let her down when I didn't want to be married to her."

Becky shook her head adamantly. "She still wants you!"

"No. She doesn't."

"How do you know?" both girls demanded.

"Because I asked. I asked her to marry me the day she had the baby. The answer was no."

Their eyes registered shock. They looked like they wanted to argue, but really, what was there to say?

Gus went to the desk by the window and picked up the letter he had written last night. He handed it to Becky.

"Give her this, will you?"

Becky took it. She looked up at him mutely, sadly, and he saw commiseration in her gaze.

"I got somethin' else for her," he said. "Out in my truck. Will you take it, too?"

"Maybe you ought to go see her. Give it to her yourself."

"No." Gus had considered that. He knew he couldn't. There was no sense in dragging this out. No sense in hanging around. "No. You two can do it for me."

He smiled a little painfully, then hefted his bag and headed for the door.

They followed him out to the truck. Mary's gift was in the cab. He scooped it up and handed it to Becky.

She stared at it, then at him, goggle-eyed.

He smiled a little crookedly. "You'll take it to her tonight?"

They both nodded. "Yes."

He tossed his duffel in the back, then came around and gave Susannah a squeeze, then gave Becky a hard hug and a kiss on the cheek. "Hope you both get a better man than me someday."

Becky tried to smile.

"Take care." Gus got into the truck and started the engine. Then he touched the brim of his hat in the time-honored cowboy salute and headed off into the sunset.

It had never looked so black.

She almost didn't answer the door.

She heard the bell and went right on reading her magazine. She didn't have to answer. She was beholden to no one. Ruthie and Jeff had left with baby Jonathan this morning. She'd taken them to the airport in Bozeman. And after she'd come home to a silent house and an empty heart.

She would fill it in time. Mary knew that.

She just needed a little space, a little quiet. Some room to heal.

"Are you sure you'll be all right?" Ruthie had asked, concern wreathing her face, just before she and Jeff and baby Jonathan had boarded the plane.

"I'll be fine," Mary had assured her. She'd been calm then. Steady. She'd even smiled brightly.

And she'd tried to keep smiling all the way home.

It didn't help that she'd had to drive over the pass she'd come over with Gus not much more than a month ago. It didn't help that she remembered what every moment of it had been like, watching him drive.

It had been clear this morning, bright and sunny. Not a snow cloud in the sky. She shouldn't have been so forcibly reminded.

But she was.

Everything, it seemed, reminded her of Gus.

And now, when the doorbell rang a second time, longer and more insistent, she dared to wonder if it might possibly be Gus.

He hadn't come with the other visitors. He hadn't stopped by on his own. He'd gone to the hospital to see Jonathan and his parents before the baby had been released—because he hadn't wanted to see her, Mary was certain.

Just as well, she'd told herself a hundred times over.

She didn't want to see him.

The door bell rang. And rang. And rang.

It sounded as if someone was leaning on it. It sounded like they wouldn't quit until she finally opened up. She drew a steadying breath, a fortifying breath and tossed aside the magazine. Then she went and opened the door.

Becky and Susannah were standing on the porch, looking awkward and nervous and worried all at once.

"We brought you a present," Susannah said.

"From Gus." And Becky stepped aside. The puppy sitting behind her looked up at Mary and wagged its entire body.

She started to cry.

"Don't!" both girls exclaimed at once.

"If you really don't want it," Susannah said urgently, "my dad said we could find a good home for it."

"But Gus got it for you. He said to give you this, too." Becky held out an envelope.

Mary took the envelope and blotted her tears with it, then crouched down so she was on the puppy's level. "Oh, baby," she murmured. "Oh, you beautiful baby!"

It was a golden retriever, maybe ten weeks old, and when Becky loosened the leash, it plunged forward and began licking the tears on her cheeks, filling her arms with its soft puppy body—Gus had known she would be aching for something to hold.

Mary buried her face in the puppy's fur. "Oh, Gus."

Everyone knew she'd be lonely. Everyone said, "Will you be okay?" But only Gus had given her something to fill the emptiness.

Only Gus.

The puppy wriggled in her embrace and finally she let it loose, let it scamper around the porch, as she stumbled to

her feet. She swiped at her eyes with the envelope once
more.

"You should maybe read it," Becky suggested.

With trembling fingers Mary did.

It was brief. To the point. Pure Gus.

Dear Mary, I thought you ought to have a friend to
keep you company. I remembered how much you
loved Arlo when I first met you. He was a great dog.
This one can be if you give him a chance. I think you
will.

I don't blame you for not trusting me. I had my
chance. I blew it a long time ago. I hurt you and I'm
sorry. I love you now more than I ever did, and I'll
never be sorry for that.

Take care. Have a good life. You deserve one.

                              Darling Augustus Holt

Mary's fingers shook. She read it again, looked at the
signature. Traced it with her finger. Then she glanced up
at the girls. "Where is he?"

"He left," Susannah said. "This afternoon."

"He went to Louisiana," Becky said. "To teach at Jim
Milburn's place."

"When will he be back?"

Becky shook her head. "Won't. Dad said he was going
to teach a workshop down there, then move on. He said
Gus told him it was better that way."

"No," Mary said, and knew it was the truth to the bottom of her soul. "It's not."

Gus had never been to Louisiana in the winter.

It was a heck of a lot nicer than in the summer. Cooler.

Drier. A nice place to visit, all in all. Except Gus had left his heart in Montana, and his brain somewhere in between.

At least that's the way it seemed.

He sure didn't seem to be making what was left of it work.

He'd come down here to give a four-day workshop on bronc riding. It wasn't difficult. He'd done it half a dozen times with Noah over the past few months. He ought to have been able to do it blindfolded. Give the guys the theory, the practice, the answers, the moves. He couldn't do anything right.

Questions baffled him. They asked him simple stuff, basic stuff, and they asked things over and over. Gus didn't hear.

He was thinking about Mary, wondering about Mary, daydreaming about Mary.

Was she all right? Was she missing Jonathan? Did she like the dog? Was a puppy too much for her? What was she doing?

"—you think, Gus?"

"—right, Gus?"

"—explain it again, Gus?"

And he would reply, "Huh? What'd you say? What?"

It wasn't only the questions he couldn't seem to focus on.

Yesterday he'd shot an entire round of practice rides, then discovered he'd never loaded the tape in the camcorder. Last night during the last round he'd pulled a cinch strap on a horse, then stood there thinking about Mary and damn near got trampled when the gate swung open and the horse blew out.

He'd do better today, he promised himself. He'd concentrate. Take it one step at a time. Focus. Really get into things.

That was why he'd decided that the hands-on approach was the best. That was why he'd decided to show a couple of guys what they were doing wrong by doing it right.

"Teach by example," Noah and Taggart always said.

Yeah, well, Gus was teaching by *bad* example.

He got distracted by a glimpse of blonde hair in the distance just as he'd settled in on the bronc and nodded his head. The gate clanged open. The horse shot out. And Gus didn't have a prayer. He got thrown. Worse, he got himself kicked in the head.

Next thing he knew Jim Milburn was hauling him to the hospital.

"Concussion," the doc said, shining a light in Gus's eyes and asking him what his name was, where he lived and who was president.

Gus thought two out of three wasn't bad. Besides he didn't really live anywhere, so his hesitation wasn't really wrong.

"Hmm," the doc said. "Gotta watch these things. No more broncs today. Take it easy."

"I gotta teach."

But the doc was adamant, and Jim agreed.

"Not this afternoon," Jim said. He took Gus back to the ranch and dropped him off at the little trailer that was his for the term of the workshop. "We'll work on somethin' else. Maybe watch *8 Seconds*. You just go on in and take it easy." He grinned. "Don't think too hard now."

"No," Gus mumbled. "I won't."

He clumped up the steps, pushed open the door and stopped right where he was.

Mary was sitting on the bed.

Did concussions cause hallucinations?

Because if they did, he was sure as hell having them.

He shut his eyes. Pressed his fingers to his temples.

Cursed the headache to end all headaches and the perversity of his brain that it would do this to him in a weak moment.

Finally he opened his eyes again.

She was still there.

"Mary?" His voice was barely a croak.

She looked at him worriedly. "They said you were hurt. They told me to wait here. Are you okay?"

Was he?

Since his hallucination could talk, Gus supposed that was good. But it might mean he was worse off than he thought. He shook his head. It hurt. He ran his tongue over his lips. "'M...fine. What're you..." He kept expecting her to vanish.

But she got up and came toward him, still smiling. "You're sure? I came to thank you for the gift."

He blinked. "Gift? Oh, yeah. You liked the dog?" She'd come halfway across the country to thank him for the dog?

"I love the dog," she said. "I named him Gus. After you."

Swell. He had a dog named after him now. And she'd come halfway across the country to tell him so. He looked at her warily. "Why?"

"Because now you won't feel obliged to name any of our sons after you."

He stared at her. His head pounded. The world spun.

What was she saying? Did she mean...

He didn't know whether to hope. He didn't know if he was dreaming.

"Mary?" he said faintly, wobbling where he stood.

She caught him as he reeled, held him and looked up into his eyes. "Ah, Gus. Darling Gus. The dog is lovely. But that's the gift I meant."

His name.

Darling Augustus. God. Even now he couldn't believe

his parents had done that to him. It didn't matter that it was a family name. It didn't matter that his fifth great-grandfather who'd borne it had been a wonderful man.

"A saint," his mother said.

"He'd have had to be," Gus had always muttered. He knew that three or four other poor souls had been stuck with it as well. It didn't matter.

It only mattered that *he* was stuck with it for his entire life. If ever there was a name you didn't want bandied about on the playground, if ever there was a name a guy could wish was as dead and buried as all his old relatives, that one was top of the list.

"Why?" he'd asked his mother, anguished.

"Why?" he'd demanded of his father more than once.

"Because you were," his mother had told him, smiling all soppy and dewy-eyed. "Just darling."

"It was a family name," his father had said stubbornly, then added almost apologetically, "An' I was in Texas buyin' horses."

Gus had threatened his brother with extinction if word got out. It was his deepest, darkest, most awful secret. He'd never told anyone. Ever.

Except now.

Except Mary.

He had trusted her with the worst truth of his life.

It had been a gift, all right.

With it he had given her the power to make his life miserable forever if she chose.

"I love you," she told him then. And she slid her arms around his waist and leaned in to kiss him.

There was no baby between them now, and it felt odd—and wonderful—to hold her so close.

"I can't seem to stop loving you," she whispered against his lips.

And Gus didn't care if his head pounded or his ears rang or what his name was. He just smiled and whispered back, "Don't."

He deepened the kiss then, damned his headache, and took the love she so graciously offered. He kissed her with a hunger so deep and so powerful that his whole body shook with the need of her. It had been so long. He loved her so much.

"Don't ever stop lovin' me, Mar'," he muttered, and if his voice broke, he didn't care. This was Mary.

He had no secrets from Mary.

Nor did she from him when she kissed him and gave him her heart, swearing, "I won't."

He was an old married man.

Well, maybe not so old. Thirty-one wasn't *that* old. But married. Oh, yeah. Gus was definitely that.

Had been for two months—ever since he and Mary had stood up right where J.D. and Lydia had and said their vows. He was well and truly married—and loving every minute of it.

Funny how what had seemed like a noose years ago was now the greatest blessing in his life.

The joy of knowing Mary was there at the end of every day, the bliss of rolling over in bed and wrapping his arms around her, the pleasure of facing her over the breakfast table in the morning—all of it—it satisfied him—*fulfilled* him. There was no other word.

He didn't hanker after the open road. He didn't flip through the road atlas and yearn for places he hadn't seen.

Because he'd seen them, Mary told him with a smile.

And that was true enough.

He also knew they didn't hold a candle to what he had right here.

He lay on the bed now and watched as Mary got ready to join him. She slipped on one of those simple cotton nightgowns that made her look innocent and virginal. It made him smile because he knew better.

He knew the fire of her passion. He knew the heat of her love.

He knew that prim virginal gown wasn't going to last more than a few minutes. But if she wanted to wear it so he could take it off, well, that was fine with him.

She raised her arms to loosen the braid of her hair, and he said, "Let me," and sat up.

She smiled at him in the mirror. "I can't believe you want to do this."

But he did. Always. There was nothing—well, *almost* nothing!—as satisfying as taking down Mary's hair.

She came to sit on the bed, and he shifted around to sit behind her. He eased the rubber band off, then ran his fingers through the braided locks, lifting them, loosening them, rubbing his hands and his face in their golden silk. He kissed her shoulders, nibbled her neck, felt her shiver.

"Gus," she protested.

"Mmm?" With his lips he caressed her ear, traced the curve of it with his tongue.

"Gus!"

"Yeah?"

"If you're going to take my hair down," she said primly, "you have to stay on task."

He groaned. "Stay on task? What is this? Even in bed you're a teacher?"

She turned her head and as she smiled he caught sight of that dimple at the corner of her mouth. "Once a teacher, always a teacher," she said. But the dimple flashed. "Besides, I'm not the only teacher. You've taught me quite a few things." She blushed at the memory of those lessons, and Gus grinned.

"I do my best," he said modestly. Picking up the hairbrush he began to run it through her hair, untangling the braid and smoothing her hair over her shoulders and down her back. He nuzzled his face in it, loving the feel of it—loving the way just being with her, combing her hair, kissing her neck made his body almost hum.

"Do I...disappoint you?" she said.

His hand stopped mid-stroke. "Disappoint me?" He was flabbergasted. "How could you possibly—?"

She shrugged almost irritably. "I'm not exactly worldly."

"Thank God."

"I'm sure there are some very nice women who are—"

"I'm sure there are," Gus cut her off. "But they're not you. I don't want anybody but you. Ever. You make me crazy. You put on those proper little gowns, and you waltz around this room like we've got all night and—"

"We do have all night."

"Well, yeah, but...well, yeah, you're right." He grinned again and tossed the hairbrush aside. He pulled her back against him into the V of his legs. "Remember when we were at Lamaze classes? Remember when I held you like this?"

"Oh—" she cleared her throat "—oh, yes." She wriggled back a little more so that her butt pressed against him.

"You really are driving me nuts," he breathed against her ear. "How can you say you're not worldly? You mean you do this naturally? You're torturing me."

Mary's head turned, and she looked at him, her eyes wide. "Torturing you?"

He bumped against her. "Yessssss."

"Oh. I see." She sounded thoughtful. "That's torture?"

"It was at Lamaze class. There was no relief, if you remember."

"I do." She shifted around so that, instead of sitting

between his legs, she sat across them. She pushed against his chest, and he tipped back flat onto the mattress. "There is now."

Gus swallowed and stared up at her with her golden hair loose and falling forward like a windblown curtain around her face. He reached for her and grasped her hips as she swung around and straddled him. Her proper nightgown bunched around her hips as she pressed down against where he needed her most.

Instinctively his hips rose, needing her closer, needing to be part of her. He took hold of the gown and, in one motion, tugged it over her head. He tossed it aside, then skimmed his hands up over her slim hips and her rib cage. He cupped her soft breasts in his hands. They were smaller now, since Jonathan's birth. He stroked them lightly and felt her shiver.

"That's torture, too," she said.

He smiled. "Sure it is."

She put her hands on his chest, drew light teasing circles around his nipples, shifted her bottom against his erection, then bent and touched each nipple with her tongue. The breath Gus hadn't known he was holding hissed through his teeth.

"Okay," he said. "You made your point."

She laughed and rose up on her knees to peel down his shorts. "And now I suppose you're going to make yours."

He groaned as he kicked his shorts away and rolled Mary beneath him, kissing her senseless and, yes, making his point at last.

She was ready for him. Eager. Drawing him down, easing him in, bringing him home.

At nineteen, home had been the last place he'd wanted to be. At thirty-one he knew better.

There was nothing better than life with Mary, no place

better than where she was. They were a pair, the two of them.

Better together, she said and he agreed, than they ever were apart.

And together now, they began to move. To love.

He kissed her lips, her nose, her cheeks, her eyelids. "Thank you," he said in a voice that shook because his body trembled with need of her. "Thank you for waiting for me. For hanging on. For being there when I finally got my act together."

"Thank you for getting it together," she whispered. "And for still caring. For becoming the man I always knew you could be."

Eyes locked, hearts beating as one, they shattered together—and became whole together. Two made one.

And after, even when they were two again—they were two together. Forever. And they lay wrapped in each other's arms and kissed softly and stroked gently.

"I love you, Mar'," he whispered.

Mary snuggled closer and rested her head against his heart. "And I love you, Darling Gus."

In the right context, Gus decided, smiling as his eyes drifted shut, it wasn't such a bad name after all.

*   *   *   *   *

Cait Blasingame needs a cowboy.
Charlie Seeks Elk needs some answers.
Working together might help them
both—or it might lead them where
neither wants to go—into each other's arms.

Find out in A COWBOY'S PROMISE
coming soon from Silhouette Desire.

Desire celebrates Silhouette's 20th anniversary in grand style!

Don't miss:

• The Dakota Man by Joan Hohl
Another unforgettable MAN OF THE MONTH
On sale October 2000

• Marriage Prey by Annette Broadrick
Her special anniversary title!
On sale November 2000

• Slow Fever by Cait London
Part of her new miniseries FREEDOM VALLEY
On sale December 2000

Plus:

FORTUNE'S CHILDREN: THE GROOMS
On sale August through December 2000
Exciting new titles from Leanne Banks, Kathryn Jensen,
Shawna Delacorte, Caroline Cross and Peggy Moreland

Every woman wants to be loved...
BODY & SOUL
Desire's highly sensuous new promotion features stories
from Jennifer Greene, Anne Marie Winston
and Dixie Browning!

Available at your favorite retail outlet.

Visit Silhouette at www.eHarlequin.com

PS20SD

You're not going to believe this offer!

In October and November 2000, buy any two Harlequin or Silhouette books and save $10.00 off future purchases, or buy any three and save $20.00 off future purchases!

Just fill out this form and attach 2 proofs of purchase (cash register receipts) from October and November 2000 books and Harlequin will send you a coupon booklet worth a total savings of $10.00 off future purchases of Harlequin and Silhouette books in 2001. Send us 3 proofs of purchase and we will send you a coupon booklet worth a total savings of $20.00 off future purchases.

Saving money has never been this easy.

I accept your offer! Please send me a coupon booklet:

Name: _____

Address: _____ City: _____

State/Prov.: _____ Zip/Postal Code: _____

Optional Survey!

In a typical month, how many Harlequin or Silhouette books would you buy <u>new</u> at retail stores?

☐ Less than 1   ☐ 1   ☐ 2   ☐ 3 to 4   ☐ 5+

Which of the following statements best describes how you <u>buy</u> Harlequin or Silhouette books? Choose one answer only that <u>best</u> describes you.

☐ I am a regular buyer and reader
☐ I am a regular reader but buy only occasionally
☐ I only buy and read for specific times of the year, e.g. vacations
☐ I subscribe through Reader Service but also buy at retail stores
☐ I mainly borrow and buy only occasionally
☐ I am an occasional buyer and reader

Which of the following statements best describes how you <u>choose</u> the Harlequin and Silhouette series books you buy <u>new</u> at retail stores? By "series," we mean books within a particular line, such as *Harlequin PRESENTS* or *Silhouette SPECIAL EDITION*. Choose one answer only that <u>best</u> describes you.

☐ I only buy books from my favorite series
☐ I generally buy books from my favorite series but also buy
     books from other series on occasion
☐ I buy some books from my favorite series but also buy from
     many other series regularly
☐ I buy all types of books depending on my mood and what
     I find interesting and have no favorite series

Please send this form, along with your cash register receipts as proofs of purchase, to:
In the U.S.: Harlequin Books, P.O. Box 9057, Buffalo, NY 14269
In Canada: Harlequin Books, P.O. Box 622, Fort Erie, Ontario L2A 5X3
(Allow 4-6 weeks for delivery) Offer expires December 31, 2000.   PHQ4002

where love comes alive—online...

eHARLEQUIN.com

shop eHarlequin

- ♥ Find all the new Silhouette releases at everyday great discounts.
- ♥ Try before you buy! Read an excerpt from the latest Silhouette novels.
- ♥ Write an online review and share your thoughts with others.

reading room

- ♥ Read our Internet exclusive daily and weekly online serials, or vote in our interactive novel.
- ♥ Talk to other readers about your favorite novels in our Reading Groups.
- ♥ Take our Choose-a-Book quiz to find the series that matches you!

authors' alcove

- ♥ Find out interesting tidbits and details about your favorite authors' lives, interests and writing habits.
- ♥ Ever dreamed of being an author? Enter our Writing Round Robin. The Winning Chapter will be published online! Or review our writing guidelines for submitting your novel.

SINTB1

If you enjoyed what you just read,
then we've got an offer you can't resist!

Take 2 bestselling love stories FREE!

Plus get a FREE surprise gift!

Clip this page and mail it to Silhouette Reader Service™

IN U.S.A.	IN CANADA
3010 Walden Ave.	P.O. Box 609
P.O. Box 1867	Fort Erie, Ontario
Buffalo, N.Y. 14240-1867	L2A 5X3

YES! Please send me 2 free Silhouette Desire® novels and my free surprise gift. Then send me 6 brand-new novels every month, which I will receive months before they're available in stores. In the U.S.A., bill me at the bargain price of $3.34 plus 25¢ delivery per book and applicable sales tax, if any*. In Canada, bill me at the bargain price of $3.74 plus 25¢ delivery per book and applicable taxes**. That's the complete price and a savings of at least 10% off the cover prices—what a great deal! I understand that accepting the 2 free books and gift places me under no obligation ever to buy any books. I can always return a shipment and cancel at any time. Even if I never buy another book from Silhouette, the 2 free books and gift are mine to keep forever. So why not take us up on our invitation. You'll be glad you did!

225 SEN C222
326 SEN C223

Name	(PLEASE PRINT)	
Address	Apt.#	
City	State/Prov.	Zip/Postal Code

 * Terms and prices subject to change without notice. Sales tax applicable in N.Y.
** Canadian residents will be charged applicable provincial taxes and GST.
   All orders subject to approval. Offer limited to one per household.
 ® are registered trademarks of Harlequin Enterprises Limited.

DES00   ©1998 Harlequin Enterprises Limited

proudly presents the exciting miniseries

MILLION DOLLAR MEN

by bestselling author
LEANNE BANKS

These super-wealthy bachelors form a secret
Millionaires' Club to make others' dreams
come true...and find the women of
their dreams in return!

EXPECTING THE BOSS'S BABY–
on sale December 2000

MILLIONAIRE HUSBAND–
on sale March 2001

THE MILLIONAIRE'S SECRET WISH–
on sale June 2001

Available at your favorite retail outlet.

Where love comes alive™

Visit Silhouette at www.eHarlequin.com   SDMDM